# Whittington

# Whittington

*By* ALAN ARMSTRONG

*Illustrated by* S. D. SCHINDLER

RANDOM HOUSE NEW YORK

NORTH SEA

SCOTLAND

IRELAND

ENGLAND

London

ENGLISH CHANNEL

FRANCE

BAY OF BISCAY

ATLANTIC OCEAN

SPAIN

Lisbon

M E

Strait of Gibraltar

A

F

R

THE HOLY
ROMAN EMPIRE

BYZANTINE
EMPIRE

BLACK
SEA

*Constantinople*

ITALY

*Palermo*

TERRANEAN SEA

*Tripoli*

C          A

**KEY**

*Dick Whittington's*
*First Voyage*        - - - - - - -

*Dick Whittington's*
*Second Voyage*      ─────────

*For Carol and Ernie, Al, the barn folks,*
*and Ben and Abby*

Published in the United States by Random House Children's Books, a division of
Random House, Inc., New York, and simultaneously in Canada by Random House of
Canada Limited, Toronto.
www.randomhouse.com/kids
*Library of Congress Cataloging-in-Publication Data*
Armstrong, Alan W. Whittington / by Alan Armstrong ; illustrated by S. D. Schindler. — 1st ed.
p. cm.
SUMMARY: Whittington, a feline descendant of Dick Whittington's famous cat of English
folklore, appears at a run-down barnyard plagued by rats and restores harmony while
telling his ancestor's story.
ISBN 0-375-82864-8 (trade) — ISBN 0-375-92864-2 (lib. bdg.) — ISBN 0-375-82865-6 (pbk.)
1. Cats—Juvenile fiction. 2. Whittington, Richard, d. 1423—Legends—Juvenile fiction.
[1. Cats—Fiction. 2. Whittington, Richard, d. 1423—Legends—Fiction.
3. Domestic animals—Fiction.] I. Schindler, S. D., ill. II. Title.
PZ10.3.A8625Wh 2005 [Fic]—dc22 2004005789
Printed in the United States of America    First Edition
10 9 8 7 6 5 4
RANDOM HOUSE and colophon are registered trademarks of Random House, Inc.

Be not forgetful to entertain
strangers: for thereby some have
entertained angels unawares.

*—Hebrews 13:2*

# CONTENTS

# Whittington

"You mean to tell me that in your family they call you Whittington?"

"No. In my family, or in what used to be my family, they called me Bent Ear. That was before my ear got torn. It used to hang over a little."

The duck nodded. "Bent Ear is more like it."

"I'm not Bent Ear anymore. My name is Whittington now," said the cat firmly. "Anyway, what's your name?"

"In Bernie's barn they call me the Lady because I'm in charge," she said, adjusting her wings. "Bernie himself calls me Muscovy, why I don't know. I'm no more from Moscow than he is, but people and cats like to make up names."

Again the cat's tail flicked and twitched, but he kept his tongue.

"So what do you want, Mr. Whittington?" asked the Lady. She settled so she was aimed into the wind and began billing her feathers to keep them lined up and fluffed. She had more than a thousand and they required a lot of care.

"A place to live."

She jerked her head around in surprise.

"You don't have a home?"

"I did," said the cat. "A boy took me in when I was

3

a kitten. Then they sent him away because he read things backwards. They were ashamed. They'd both been to college and graduate school and here they had a child who couldn't read. They sent him to a special school out west. They said it was the best thing. He was going to take me along but they said no."

His voice trailed off.

"And?" the duck asked gently.

"They never loved me," the cat said, looking away. "When the weather got cool, the man started jogging in leggings. I'd be waiting by the door when he got back. If I brushed his leg, he'd get a shock. He'd kick, I'd bite.

"With their boy gone, they began to wonder why they should care for his cat. When I got into a fight and killed the tom next door, they threw me out. Or they wouldn't let me in again, which comes to the same thing."

The duck gave him a long look. "Is that how you got your ear, fighting?"

The cat nodded. "It drooped before. He tore it half off. Then he bit me in the neck. Must have hit a nerve. That's why I weave. I can't help it."

"What did you fight about?" asked the Lady.

"Love, a female, principle, religion, it's all the same."

"No, it is not!" said the Lady sharply. She had strong views about romance and dreamed of love. "But I don't see why fighting should get you thrown out. That's what tomcats do. Everybody knows that. I think you're well rid of that family. Lucky they didn't have you put down."

"If they'd tried they'd have paid in blood."

"Yes," said the Lady after a pause. "The senior barn rat is one-eyed now from the pecking he got when they ganged up on the gray rooster. I'd have said that rooster was a dandy and a coward, but when you're fighting for your life you'll risk everything."

She gave a shudder, her way of shaking something unpleasant from mind.

"Why don't you try for another family, wait and meow by a neighbor's door and see if they'll take you in?"

"Because I'm not cute anymore," said Whittington. "My voice is harsh, I've got the shakes, I have opinions, I like to stay out, I stink, I like to fight. I'm not a house pet."

The Lady nodded. "I guess not."

The wind picked up. The Lady shifted into it like a moored dory. She waited for the cat to speak but he didn't. Snow was coming. She wanted to get to her bath.

"So what do you want from me?" she asked.

"A place in the barn."

She cocked her head.

"Why don't you just take it?"

"I want to be part of the talking. If I'd snuck in, the chickens would have been afraid and maybe you too. I didn't want that. I want friends."

He paused. The Lady didn't say anything.

"I can help out," he added. "I'm a good ratter."

"Really?" said the duck, leaning forward. "Most cats are afraid of rats."

"It's my specialty."

"That I'd like to see. They just killed one of my friends."

She shuddered again. "Enough of that!"

The Lady heaved herself up and flexed her wings. They were large. For a moment she towered over the cat.

"I'll have to ask the others," she said as she headed to the pond.

## 2

# The Animals in the Barn

THE HORSES KNEW SNOW was coming. They curved their hoofs and dug bowls in the dust, where they lay down and rolled for a last good bath. It's surprising how dust cleans hair and soothes itches. Lice and fleas can't abide it.

The horses inspired the chickens to dry-clean too. They had their own dust pits, where they flapped and stretched as if they were airing bedding.

Coraggio the rooster was the singer. The bantams only murmured until someone laid an egg; then they all squawked together as hard as they could because chickens are socialists and it's one for all in the world of eggs. The Lady could hiss but there seemed to be no music in her. She had never laid an egg.

Dogs and coyotes preyed on the fowl. Hawks were a threat too, along with the occasional fox, skunk, and raccoon. The biggest threat was rats. Bernie said he would put down poison to make them bleed to death inside, but he was afraid the chickens would get it. They ate everything. The mice did too, but nobody thought about them. The other reason Bernie didn't try poison was that poisoned rats go into their holes to die and the stench is intolerable.

When one of the hens felt an egg coming, she would scratch out a nest in one of the topmost hay bales, preen herself of extra feathers to line it, and settle down to brood. Sometimes the rats found her. They always found the chicks. Bantams who weren't sitting on eggs roosted high up on the roof rafters to keep away from the rats. The bantams could fly.

When dusk came, Coraggio would flap and claw his way up to a high place on the bales. He couldn't fly because his wings had been clipped. To keep their birds from flying away, farmers sometimes clip off the final wing segments on young fowl. They never grow back. Coraggio's wings had been clipped before Bernie got him. Every day after feeding the horses Bernie made sure some bales were stepped so Coraggio could get up to a safe place.

The Lady's wings had been clipped too. She had a hollowed-out place near the door where she could keep an eye on things. Her wings were big and powerful even though they'd been clipped. She could knock a rat silly. They knew this. She was in charge in the barn.

It was a curious thing, the Lady's authority. The horses obeyed her, along with everyone else except the rats. What gave her power was how steady she was. She never rushed; she was always sure, she took responsibility. When something came up, she said what to do. Presence of mind counts for a lot in this world. The Lady was as confident of her judgment as she was of her beauty. Nothing so improves the appearance as a good opinion of oneself.

# 3

# Bernie and How He Got the Horses

THE FARM ROAD ran off the state highway past a house and down to Bernie's barn. It was steep, muddy, and slippery, for all the gravel he put down. Every spring and fall the rains washed it out. In winter it got so slick he couldn't get the truck down; he had to slip-slide in to feed and water the animals. By Christmas, when ice had locked up the pump, he'd clamber down behind his grandkids' sled with jugs of warm water.

The road ended in the barnyard. The pond was to the left. On warm nights you could hear peepers and frogs and the horses snorting and talking together. Beginning at four in the morning you'd hear Coraggio. He crowed ancient music in a high, four-beat whoop that ended with a sound like scraping metal. His music always awakened Marker, the dog that lived in the house on the hill. Marker would listen and moan.

Bernie was a tall, lanky man with a face like Lincoln's and a dead cigar stub in his mouth. He wasn't allowed to smoke in the house; his truck was his smoking room. It smelled of independence. Even when he wasn't in it, it had a rich smell of cigars. He didn't talk much. He was so spare his jeans looked about to fall off. Under the baseball cap that said TEXACO, his hair was gray and wavy. He had a temper and a high voice you could hear a long way off when he was mad.

His barn used to be a tobacco shed. Pieces of land had been sold off from the farm before he got it, so there wasn't enough left for a tobacco crop. There was space for a paddock, though.

He had always wanted horses. He didn't know why, he just liked them. He liked the way they looked, the way they moved, their smell. He could watch horses for hours. There was something beautiful about the way they stood motionless in the sun, one hoof cocked up. He liked the curve of a horse's foot, the delicate way they never stepped on a giddy chicken or a small child. He liked their neighing and nickering. He'd never had horses, he didn't know how to ride, he didn't know what it would take to keep them; but when he ended up with a place that had a barn and some ground, he decided to try the company of horses. His daughter's passing away had left him lonely in a way he'd never been before.

When the county agricultural agent showed up at his gas station, Bernie told him about the barn and his dream of horses. A few days later the agent came back with a horse-care book and showed him in the *Gazette*'s classifieds where two retired Arabian racers were offered for one hundred dollars. They'd been stable mates for a long time. The buyer would have to take both. It wasn't a lot of money. Bernie didn't ask Marion, his wife.

Bernie called about the horses. The man selling them said if they didn't go soon, he'd have to let the knackers take them for horsemeat. "What can I do?" he said in a broken voice. "I've sold my place, I have to clear out."

The gelding named Aramis was twenty-four. Li'l Spooker, the female, was twenty-eight. Old for horses, but they were in good shape. They had vet papers and the farrier had them on his list so he knew to come around when they needed new shoes or had to have their teeth filed. The man warned Bernie that they'd never been trained to the saddle. That was okay with Bernie; he hadn't been either. Bernie understood everything the man said except the part about filing teeth. He bought the horses. He forgot about filing their teeth.

The man who sold them didn't have a horse van and Bernie didn't either. The day after he paid he was working out how he might walk them up a ramp and tie them down in his pickup when Ted from Wools and Furs showed up at the Texaco with a vanload of llamas.

Ted agreed to haul the horses in exchange for gas. He would have done it for nothing because Bernie was always doing things for him. Bernie helped everybody but it was hard to get him to take anything in return. He liked making his own way.

Ted was a huge Cornishman. Like most giants, he was gentle, especially with animals. His voice was not like anyone else's because there were no pauses between his words. He ran everything together in a song heavy with the accent of his seacoast home in the southwest of England.

He and Bernie rode over together to get the horses. The seller was outside with them when the van pulled up. He tried to smile but he couldn't. He handed over the bridles and stumbled to his house. Ted lowered the walkup. He sang softly to the horses, calling Spooker "my grand old girl" and Aramis "my brave, good boy" as he guided first one, then the other, up the ramp. When they balked, he didn't shove; he cajoled with his music and his immense paws.

The horses stayed tied up in the barn while Bernie and Al, the night man at the Texaco, fenced the paddock and went to the hay man's. The horses were scared. Everything was strange. There had been horses in the barn before, it was fitted with stalls, but that was a long time ago. It smelled of tobacco, old hay, and things left behind. Birds flitted in and out, barn swallows, a phoebe. The phoebe was busy with a nest of fledglings high up over the horses. The swallows wheeled and played in shafts of light as they called to one another. Sparrows darted up close, curious about the newcomers and pleased with their droppings. Just outside, a white-throated sparrow sang. The birds were comforting. The way the beams and stanchions were worn smoothed the edge of newness. It was not an unfriendly place. The horses were thirsty. When the men came back, they brought water. Once they began stacking the green bales it began to smell like home.

# 4

## Abby and Ben Meet the Horses

BERNIE AND AL were away from the station all day. By then his customers knew they were off getting horses. Marion and the two grandchildren knew too. In a small town word gets around.

Abby was ten; her brother, Ben, was eight. They were fair, round-faced kids with big white teeth their faces hadn't grown into yet. Abby was tall. She stood straight, so she looked older than her years. She had a blaze of gold hair. Ben was sturdy; his hair was darker, buzz-cut. Until the horses came the kids were solemn. They lived with Bernie and Marion. Their mother was dead. They didn't know where their father was.

The morning after the horses arrived, Bernie went out to his truck at five o'clock to go feed them. Abby and Ben were sitting in it, waiting. They said they'd help. The horses were prancing around the paddock with tails flying when the truck reached the top of the hill. The kids were as excited as the horses. Everybody was smiling. Inside the barn it smelled of fresh hay and horse.

That afternoon Bernie bought brushes and curry-combs at the Agway, and a stepladder so the kids could do the horses' backs. After a couple of days the horses began to smell like the children and the children began to smell like the horses. Abby and Ben rode over with Bernie every morning at five to help muck, feed, and water. Before the horses arrived it was hard to get the kids up for the school bus at seven. Now they had friends who needed them. Sometimes when the kids doled out the sticky grain with molasses and vitamins, the horses would nuzzle and lick them, probably for salt but maybe for love. There is nothing softer or more delicate than a horse's muzzle. Sometimes if Bernie was standing close by, they'd nuzzle him too. "Go on!" he'd mutter as he pushed them off, but it made him smile. His years fell away when he smiled. You could see the boy he'd been.

5

# The Lady Tells the Barn About Whittington

AS SOON AS BERNIE drove away, the rats would rush from their holes, chittering and squealing, to chase the Lady and the chickens from the grain. They made off with all the bantam eggs they could find. One night they cornered the deckled gray and killed him for the food in his craw, tore him open and left him in a mess of blood and feathers. The Lady had nightmares that she'd be next because her wings were clipped and she moved slow. There were rat holes in the barn walls and tunnels in the back part, where it was dark.

The morning she met the cat, as soon as she finished her bath the Lady went and told the other animals about Whittington. She didn't giggle about his name or mention his old one. She'd heard enough of his story to understand why he'd given it up.

The bantams churred and scolded at the idea of a cat moving in. "Cats eat birds," the oldest one said. "We have enough problems with the rats."

Coraggio was opposed too. "No more predators," he declared.

There was an approving murmur from the bantams. The horses didn't pay much attention. They'd known cats before, never had much to do with them. The rats crept out to listen. They didn't have a vote, but they held with the horses until the Lady spoke again.

"Whittington says he's a ratter. I don't know, but that's what he says. He looks like a fighter. We could use a ratter," she added, glaring in the direction of the rats. There was an "Ooh!" of approval from the fowl.

The Lady reminded the horses how close they'd come to ending up dog food. It was the same with the rooster and the bantams; they'd been remnants at a livestock auction. The auctioneer had announced that if no one took them, he'd wring their necks, he wasn't going to interrupt his weekend on their account. So somebody bid a dollar, borrowed a crate, and left them at Bernie's. Bernie had a reputation. You could tell from his smile and the way he walked he was likelier to say yes than no to a crate of tired chickens.

The barn hummed with talk about the cat. Not the moving-in part, they couldn't stop him from doing that. The family part. You can't get rid of somebody once he's part of your family. Whatever happens, you're responsible. But who could say who belonged in or out of that family?

What clinched it for Whittington was Ben and Abby looking around the barn at five the next morning and asking in unison, "Where's the cat?"

Bernie looked up. "What cat?"

# 6

## The Animals Tell Whittington About Themselves

WHITTINGTON WAS WAITING under the hedge. It was ticking snow. He stepped out when he saw the Lady.

"Okay," she said. "We'll go down together. I'll introduce you."

When they arrived, it was snug in the barn, pungent with damp dung and hay. The bantams murmured and cackled together like they were telling jokes. Now and then, Coraggio crowed. He always startled folks when he crowed because they never knew when he'd do it, and he didn't either.

The Lady and Whittington sat close in the hay talking about themselves and the news about Bernie's selling out. Every winter Bernie talked about selling out because he had arthritis in his knee. The cold weather made it hurt. It was more and more painful for him to climb down and up the hill when it was too icy for the truck.

The animals were all worried about moving. Talk about moving is like talk about divorce, nobody knows what it will mean except that everything will be different and not better. Who but Bernie would shelter and feed two old horses and an assortment of odd birds?

As the snow thickened, the Lady told Whittington her story. She'd been one of twelve ducklings that Bernie got one Easter. A stranger had showed up at the Texaco with a crate of ducks. He said he was going to drop them in the trash if Bernie didn't take them.

The fox had made off with a couple of the Lady's brothers right away. The hawk took one, the rats took a toll, so did the raccoon and some coyotes. She was the only duck left.

"Aramis and Li'l Spooker were racehorses," the Lady explained, as if they weren't standing there. "Aramis is a gelding. He was fast, but Spooker won purses. Aramis never finished in the money. Spooker won't let him forget it."

"What's a gelding?" the cat wanted to know.

"It's an operation they do to manage male horses. Otherwise he'd be wild."

Aramis looked away.

"Because she won money, Spooker goes first for everything around here. The hay goes down, Spooker gets the first bite. Water in the bucket, her muzzle is right in there sucking it down. It's the same when Bernie or one of the kids tosses out the grain and cracked corn with molasses, Spooker gets the first.

"Bernie puts down grain for me and the other birds. We have to hurry to eat it, though. The rats hassle us. They're aggressive. Norways, they call themselves, but what they have to do with Norway I don't know. 'Brown rat' is a good enough name for them.

"Despite the Moscow in my name, my ancestors were English," she continued, swelling up some, the way people do who have ties to Great Britain. "There's a college in England where they honor my line by marching around behind a duck held aloft on a pole. It has to do with the wings of knowledge."

At this point the Lady gave a great flap to show the wings of knowledge. Her wings went out as far as you could stretch your arms.

Coraggio roused himself and flapped too. He was a Plymouth Rock, white with a red crown. He sang all day on the dung heap but he kept himself as clean as the president in his white starched shirt.

"I got my name because of my bravery," he said. "It was the night of the raccoon. She slipped in looking for eggs. She came after me, thought I was a hen. I drove her off. When Bernie came in the morning and saw the feathers, he figured what happened. He said I had courage. I took it from there.

"Our family is descended from the wild red jungle fowl," he continued. "In science we're called *Gallus gallus*. We are the most important bird in the world. Wherever men go we go too because of our eggs. Men have kept us by them for four thousand years."

He didn't mention drumsticks.

There was a ruckus among the bantams.

Coraggio *ahem*ed. "Because of *their* eggs. But I keep things going. Some of them can do an egg every other day."

The cat looked around for an egg.

"There aren't any right now," said the senior bantam. "We're too busy keeping warm. Wait until there's more sun."

The Lady turned to the horses. "Your turn."

Spooker said that she and Aramis were Arabians. Their ancestors had been brought here when America was a new world. "The Spaniards brought us in their ships because we're the fastest ones. Other breeds can pull heavier loads, but we're the fastest. In the Westerns they ride Arabians like us. We're professionals. A big woman raised and trained us on dirt roads in the mountains in Vermont. She taught us to pull a sulky, a bare-frame cart with two wheels and a seat. The races were on level ground. Our drivers wore bright silks and helmets. They were all skinny, easy to pull. They carried whips to snap for signals, not to hit us. You don't run a whole race flat out; there's strategy in racing. That's what I mean about our being professionals—we knew to follow the signals. We raced around a track with grandstands where people stood cheering. The cheering always made us speed up. I won purses, prize money."

Aramis made a loud noise that wasn't a sneeze. He didn't like being reminded that he'd never finished in the money. "There were more horses around before there were cars and trucks," he said. "A hundred years ago even old horses like us were everything on a farm—truck, tractor, transportation. Horses don't have work like that anymore. We're pets. We're helping Bernie raise his grandkids."

Whittington just listened. He could have mentioned that the word "cat" is found in various languages as far back as they can be traced.

The one-eyed rat they called the Old One stayed quiet too. For his part he could have told an interesting tale about his ancestors arriving at Jamestown with Captain John Smith and, long before that, rats coming to Europe from China and the plague they carried. Men bring rats along wherever they go. They don't mean to; the rats that travel with men travel as stowaways. The fleas and the Black Death were both stowaways on the rats. He might have mentioned that in India the rat is the companion of Ganesha, the beloved god with the elephant's head.

The Old One didn't speak because he was sizing up the cat. He'd never seen a cat before but he'd heard about them. It was the way this cat wove from side to side that worried him, like a snake ready to strike. The Old One knew about snakes. Snakes ate rats.

# 7

## Havey and the Cat's Surprise

BERNIE HAD A GUARD DOG at the Texaco. Every noon, when he drove out to the barn to water the animals, he'd bring Havey along so she could have a run and do her business. Her favorite thing was to chase the Lady and nip at the horses. Bernie always yelled but it was a halfhearted yell because this was Havey's only exercise. To tell the truth, it was the horses' only exercise too. The rest of the day they stood around in the paddock and she sat chained up behind the Texaco.

The Lady warned Whittington about Havey. "She'll kill if she can. She has scores to settle. She lives to get even.

"I heard Bernie tell the hay man how he got her," she continued. "'One afternoon,' he said, 'I saw this dog wandering around in the churchyard across from the Texaco. She looked lost. Real skinny, like she'd just had puppies, teats hanging down. There'd been some drifters hanging around. I figure they kept the puppies and dumped her. I brought her some meat. She snarled but she took it. She was starved. Next day I brought some more. Called the dog officer. He took her away. I felt bad about what might happen to her at the pound, so I called and said if nobody claimed her I'd take her. Nobody called. A couple of days later I brought her back to the Texaco. She's too much of a biter to take home, so she lives chained up out back. Keeps people away from the broken-down cars. Had her fixed so she wouldn't have any more puppies.'"

Whittington listened carefully. "An odd name, Havey," he said. "Where did she get it?"

The Lady gave him a look. "She's proud of it," she said. "It's the name of a motor oil. Havey says her full name—Havoline—used to be on posters in gas stations. It was famous."

Havey left her scat around. That helped keep the coyotes away, and the fox. When Havey visited, the rats lay low.

One windy morning before Whittington arrived, the Lady was in her bathing place and didn't hear the truck when Bernie stopped at the top of the hill. Havey raced down and caught her unawares. She got some of her tail feathers and all of her dignity as the Lady squalled into the pond.

Havey had rushed the cat a couple of times too and sent him up a tree, but it was her daily assaults on the Lady that made the cat mad. That had to stop. He and the Lady made a plan. The Lady would wait for Havey near the barn door. Instead of rushing into the pond, which is what she usually did, the duck was to dive under the barn door. They practiced. She just fit. The risk was that she wouldn't be fast enough. Whittington rehearsed her. He was the dog. He zipped up, she shot under. She could make it.

Their plan was that once she got Havey close to the barn Whittington would give the dog a surprise.

By the time they heard Bernie's truck the next morning, everybody was wound up tight. The horses were tearing around the paddock, the Lady was flapping in front of the barn, Coraggio was crowing, the bantams were yawping. It was melee time.

Havey hit the ground before the truck stopped rolling. Bernie swore as she tore after the duck, but no more than he usually did. The Lady let the dog get just close enough before she dove.

Then there was a screech that made Bernie's hair go up. From the beam over the barn door something dropped like lightning. What followed was like a bronco rider going bareback on a wild horse.

Whittington had landed on Havey's back just as the dog tasted the tip ends of the Lady's tail feathers. The cat locked his jaws on an ear, planted his front claws deep in the dog's shoulders, and with his hinders he kicked out hair in tufts so thick you'd think he was trying to dig a hole back there. The dog's bark shifted from fury to terror. She rolled over. Whittington jumped clear.

Havey was big and tough but she was out of shape, like the football player who was very good years ago but has mostly sat down since.

She made a run at Whittington. The cat would let her get just so close, then he'd dance aside. Havey was used to cats that ran. On a straight-out run she had a chance of getting what she went after, but this cat didn't run. The dog made another pass. This time Whittington met her head-on with a pawful of claws. Havey gave that cat a death bite that would have done in a football. The cat seemed to be all hair and air. The dog ended up with a mouthful of fur. Her nose felt like she'd met the business end of a porcupine. She'd had enough.

It didn't take a minute and Bernie was there the whole time, kicking at the cat, kicking at the dog, missing everything, yelling and cursing. He lost his cigar. When it was over, he locked Havey in the pickup and spent the next half hour quieting the horses so he could barrow out their manure without getting run over.

When she heard the truck door slam, the Lady came out.

"Thank you," she said to the cat. "I always wanted to do that."

"I do like a fight," said Whittington, "but they cost me." He had bare places on his thigh and tail where Havey had given him the death bite.

It was Christmas before the hair on Havey's back grew in. The cat carried his patches to Valentine's Day.

After the fight, the cat no longer wove from side to side. Whittington figured it was the flip he did when Havey bit him.

"Chiropractory," the Lady said, nodding firmly. "A good snap works every time."

# 8

# The Last Day for Baths

THERE'D BEEN SNOW, then there was a string of mild days before winter finally slammed the door. It was so still you could hear the freight train a half mile away. Northfield is an ancient lake bed, a fertile pudding of fine silt: tap it hard at one place and it jiggles. The noon freight grumbling its way made the barn dance a little.

It had just passed when Whittington was started out of his doze by yells and clacking and the horses tearing around.

The Lady was unperturbed.

"It's the crows," she said. "They come over here to show off, twenty or thirty of them. Their yelling reminds the horses of what the race crowd sounded like, so they run. They can't help themselves."

The Lady waddled to her special place in the road, squatted, then flapped hard, sending up silt and worn-out feathers. She paused and rested like a movie star in her bubble bath, then did it again. When she finished, she billed and preened her luxuriance. In the sunlight her black tail feathers glistened purple like oil on water.

Whittington took a bath too, paws in air, twisting and rubbing on his back to scratch some places he couldn't reach. When he stood up, he shook out a small cloud. He stretched and yawned. It was surprising how wide he could open his mouth. His upper and lower fangs were long and narrow, skim-milk white.

The animals knew it was the last day for baths. Spooker ambled to the far side of the paddock near her standing-still place. She pawed the dirt to get things ready, then in one easy motion she went to her knees and rolled on her side, switching and kicking like a puppy. When she stood, she snorted mightily and gave herself a tremendous, dusty shake.

Later, the ducks went over, headed south in long, ragged V's, yelling encouragement to one another. The Lady and the cat watched with admiration. Their calls made the Lady restless; those were her kinfolk. She didn't really want to join them, though. The barn was her home. She couldn't fly anyway.

The crows had settled next door to glean the corn-field. There was excited calling back and forth, whees and caws and all the other voices crows make. The cat

and the duck went to investigate. Crows stick together like rats. One crow always keeps watch. Gregory, the watch crow, yelled alarm and with the others drove them off. The crows were only half the Lady's size, but they dove and pecked. The Lady hustled back to the barnyard with Whittington close behind. Then, because the sun was warm and they had pictures in mind to doze over and a friend close by, they slipped under the tangle of blackberry whips to be safe from hawks and took a snooze.

**9**

# The Lady Asks Whittington
# to Tell His Story

AS WINTER CAME ON, it got colder. The Lady's pond froze solid and the ground got so hard there wasn't much for the chickens to scratch. The winds got sharper. Only on still afternoons would the horses go stand in the sun for an hour. When the big snow finally came, everyone was shut up in the barn. They were bored. The Lady turned to Whittington. "You said your name is in history. Tell us the story."

The cat was pleased to be asked. He had a deep voice. The horses leaned close to hear. From the rustlings around you could tell that every ear in the barn was listening.

"When I was growing up, the boy in my home . . ."

Whittington choked up, remembering the boy he'd loved. Coraggio fluttered noisily to straighten a feather. The duck looked away. The horses snorted; they understood.

The three young rats snickered. The Old One cuffed them so hard they went sprawling.

"Listen to your blood enemy and you may learn enough to save your lives," he hissed.

"My boy," the cat continued, "told me about a Christmas pageant at his school, 'Dick Whittington and His Marvelous Cat.' Whittington was English. He lived a hundred years before Columbus. The thing is, I'd already heard about him and his cat before from my mother. I am descended from Dick Whittington's cat.

"Dick Whittington was a merchant. He traded the woolens of England for the finest fabrics from all over the world—silks from China and India, brocades and taffetas from Spain, velvets, damasks. He grew rich. He left his money for a college, libraries, a hospital, and an almshouse where the poor could rest and get food. He saw to the laying of pipe and setting up spigots to bring clean water to the slums. He knew what it was to be poor.

"He owed his fortune to his cat."

"What was the cat's name?" the Lady asked.

"Nobody knows," said Whittington. "History records the names of men because men write it. Dick Whittington's name survives but his cat's name is lost. That's what's wrong with history. If it hadn't been for his cat, no one would remember Dick. Now no one remembers his cat."

Suddenly Whittington slipped into the shadows like smoke.

There was a long silence; then the cat screamed as he had the morning he flew at Havey. There was a thud and a thrashing noise that slowly faded. Then they heard the high, sharp shriek of death.

Whittington came back with a rat in his jaws. His front paw was bloody. He laid the rat at the Lady's feet.

"Bravo," she said grimly. "Eleven to go." Then she looked down at the soft brown body and imagined the barn without rats. There were four red dots on the pelt.

They heard Bernie's truck and Havey's yelling. They heard the kids. The kids had a snow day. They were underfoot at the Texaco, so Bernie had brought them along.

Abby and Ben had carrots for the horses, canned milk and tuna for the cat. They saw the dead rat and called Bernie.

"Don't touch it," he said. "I'll get rid of it outside."

While Bernie unloaded, the kids put down extra grain for the Lady and the chickens and doled out carrots and sugar cubes to the horses. Whittington circled around, waiting for his treat. There was a problem: no can opener.

"That's okay," said Whittington, "I'll have rat."

Abby took the cans to Bernie. He opened them with his knife. The kids fed the cat tuna with their fingers, then filled the empty can with milk. The three of them ended up smelling like tuna.

"This is better than rat," said Whittington, licking up the last bits. "Rat is tough and gamy."

Ben reached over to pet him. Whittington was startled; then, almost inaudible, came an uneven rumble.

"You can purr too!" Abby exclaimed.

"Doesn't sound like you've done it for a while," Ben said. "You're out of practice."

The cat smiled, stretching out his toes and rumbling away.

## 10

## The Man Whittington Named
## Himself After

BERNIE HAD TO LEAVE while he could still get the
truck up. The kids wanted to stay. He said okay. Abby
had a watch; he'd collect them at three by the highway.

They could hear the storm. The wind sent flakes in
through the cracks and the broken-out window up top.
Ben shivered. The Lady had the kids pull down fresh
hay. It fluffed up and smelled like summer. She made the
horses lie down close together and had the kids snuggle
next to them. She settled herself on one fluff, Coraggio
on another. The bantams made a show of flying up to
the rafters and perching where they could look over
everything in comfort.

The cat was full of tuna and canned milk. He
wanted to lie down in a warm place too. The Lady told
him to get up on the stall railing where everybody could
see him.

"Now go on with your story," she said.

"Story? What story?" the kids chorused.

Whittington shook himself. "This is the story of rats and the cats that hunt them. Rats carry the fleas that carry plague. Plague makes your groin and underarms swell up and your tongue turn black. You get buboes and spots and foam at the mouth and die in agony. It's called the Black Death.

"Dick Whittington's cat won him a fortune because she was a rat-hunter. Centuries before they figured out what plague was and how it spread, people knew that a good rat-hunter could save your life.

"The man I'm named for was born about the time the Black Death hacked through England like a filthy knife. By the time he was five years old a quarter of his town was empty. It was a horrible loneliness.

"His family was poor. The soil was thin and ill-tended. There wasn't enough food. There were no schools. The grandmother who lived with his family taught him to read. The priest had taught her. There were no printed books. She copied out things on scraps of stiffened cloth and scraped animal skins called parchments. She wrote down remedies, recipes, family records, and Bible passages the priest taught her.

"She smelled of the oils, herbs, and mint she used in the remedies she made. She was a midwife and a healer, one of the cunning folk they called her. The priest taught her reading and writing so she could copy recipes for remedies and keep the parish records. Dick gathered simples for her. He had a good eye. That was his work. Other boys his age picked stones from fields, gleaned corn, scared crows, drove geese. If you were idle, you didn't eat."

"What are simples?" the Lady wanted to know. The kids nodded. They didn't know either.

"Plants," the cat said. "They made medicine then from leaves and blossoms, sap, roots. Dick's grandmother boiled and ground plants into ointments and syrups to heal people."

"We fowl do that," the Lady said, looking at Coraggio. "When we're ill, we know what to eat to get better."

"We do too," said Abby. "When we're sick to the stomach, Gran makes tea from the mint that grows around, and stuff for hurts from tansy, the plant with yellow button flowers."

"For colds she makes yarrow tonic and rose-hip paste," said Ben. "She puts honey in the tonic. The rose stuff is bitter."

"When I'm sick, I eat new grass," the cat said.

"Okay," said the Lady. "Go on with your story."

"Dick was always surprised how warm his grandmother was when they sat close together. She read aloud the same things over and over, leading with her finger as she sounded out the letters. What he read to himself at first was what he remembered hearing as he followed her hand. He'd mouth the words as he went along, sounding them out. Not many of his time knew how to read and few of those learned silent reading. He was a mumbling reader all his life.

"One afternoon in the village he saw a gold coin. He'd been loitering around a stout stranger, hoping to perform some service and earn a tip, when the man went into the baker's. Dick followed him in and watched as the stranger bought a halfpenny's worth of bread. The stranger got three round wheat loaves, honey-colored and heavy. He stuffed two into his coat and gave one to the boy. The man fumbled in his purse for a coin. He held it out for Dick to see. It was the size of a fingernail, stamped with a face. It gleamed like nothing Dick had ever seen before. What impressed him almost as much as its gleam was how carefully the baker studied it and weighed it and how many coins he gave in change.

"Then one day outside the inn he overheard a carter telling the men helping him unload barrels of cider that he had heard from a man who had been there that London's streets were paved with gold and all the people were plump and healthy.

"That night Dick had a dream. He dreamed he went to London and became the stout stranger, filling his purse with the small, gleaming rounds of gold that lay like pebbles in the streets. He went to the baker and stuffed his pockets, he went to the inn and was served roast meat and cider. In his dream he was never hungry again. He wore warm clothes and was never cold again either.

"He had heard talk that he was to be put in service to a tanner, a hard man who beat his boys and fed them poorly. Working with hides was a dirty, stinking business. The boys had to scrape off rotting flesh and hair and lift the heavy skins in and out of the tanbark vats. A boy in the tanner's service had hawked up blood and died. Dick figured he'd better get out on his own pretty quick."

## II

# Dick's Dream

THE HORSES SHUFFLED. They needed to go out for a few minutes. The bantams fluttered, the Lady took some water. Whittington was hungry. Dick's dream of roast meat made him think of food. Then everybody came back and settled and the cat resumed.

"Every morning on awakening, Dick told himself his dream to keep courage. He didn't think about what he would be leaving, only where he was going. 'London' rang in his head like a bell.

"No carriages passed through his town. The farmers' carts never went much beyond the village. The boy watched and waited for another stranger to come through. He knew he'd get to London somehow. He knew his dream was a prophecy."

"What's prophecy?" Ben asked.

"It's telling about what's going to happen," the cat replied. "As part of her learning to read, the boy's grandmother had copied out Bible prophecies with the priest."

"How did you learn to read?" Ben asked. He wanted to know because he was having trouble.

"I never learned," said Whittington. "Do you know how?"

"Some," said the boy.

"No he doesn't, not really," said Abby, shaking her head. She didn't say it in a mean way; she said it with the worry of love.

"Gran got a note from his teacher that he's not reading like he's supposed to. They're going to put him in Special Ed if he doesn't get better."

Ben's face darkened.

The Lady looked up angrily. "Who is Special Ed?"

"It's not a person," Abby said. "It's a class they take you to so you don't hold up the others. They take you out of the room and everybody knows you're stupid. They call the Special Eds 're-tards.'"

Whittington studied Ben's face, remembering another boy.

"Do you know how to read?" the cat asked Abby.

She nodded. "Gran helped me."

What she didn't say was that after her mother died Abby wouldn't do anything in school. It was a battle to get her to go at all. Finally Marion started taking her. So long as her gran sat in the classroom Abby would work along with the others, but she was way behind. If Gran left, Abby fought and cried. Marion quit doing the books and car rentals at the Texaco and signed on as a teacher's aide.

"Imagine me, with no college, helping out in a classroom," she told Bernie. "I'll tell you, those teachers are heroes, all what they do." The kids assigned to Marion—Abby and two of her classmates—were struggling and angry. There's a lot of anger in not being able to do what people think you should be doing. Marion's job was to help them read the special books they'd been assigned. She brought in gingerbread men she made with a lot of ginger; she gave pats and pushes. As they progressed from one book to the next, she'd tell them, "Look what you did!"

The Lady asked Abby, "Why doesn't your gran help Ben the way she helped you?"

"He won't let her. She gives him a book or even a cereal box to read and he throws it across the room. He does the same thing in school sometimes."

Ben looked down. He was scared. Reading was too hard. It was the hardest thing he'd ever tried. Reading aloud meant dragging words out, even easy words. He'd get three words right, then there'd be a baffler. There were giggles when he missed. His reading aloud was flat, just words. If the teacher asked him about what he'd read, he'd shrug. He was ashamed. He learned best watching and listening. If he could see something done, he could do it. But writing and arithmetic—things got blurred and turned around. Sometimes the word he read didn't make sense, or it wasn't a real word at all. The marks didn't read for him the way they did for others. In arithmetic he got a different answer, or no answer. There was a bigger and bigger gap between his world and everybody else's.

"Do you?" the cat asked him.

"Do I what?" asked the boy, startled out of his reverie.

"Throw the things they give you to read?"

He didn't say anything.

The Lady looked hard at Abby. "Could you help Ben like your grandmother helped you?"

"He wouldn't let me," Abby said.

"Oh, yes he would!" said the Lady, flexing her huge wings and taking charge.

"Wouldn't you?" the Lady asked, giving Ben a meaningful look.

He nodded a small nod.

"But he sees backward," said Abby. "You need a specialist to fix that. It isn't glasses. They checked him for glasses. I had a hearing problem, so I couldn't read at first either. I had earaches. Even when I didn't have earaches, I couldn't hear the sounds of some of the letters. *W* and *r* sounded the same to me, so 'white' and 'right' sounded the same. They were going to send me out until I fell down the stairs. I went to the hospital for an operation on my ears. It fixed my balance and I heard better. The specialist helped me get the sounds of the letters. The night I was in the hospital Mom sat up with me so I wouldn't be scared. . . ." She broke off.

The Lady coughed and looked at Ben.

"Do you hear okay?"

"Yeah."

"Do you see me backward?"

"No. . . ."

"Okay," said the Lady, turning to Abby. "Tomorrow bring the book."

"Which one?"

"There's more than one book?"

Abby nodded.

"Whittington, what book did Dick learn from?"

"His grandmother didn't have a book," said the cat. "She taught from what the priest had helped her write down. She wrote on scraps. Dick learned the Bible sayings and parables the old woman had copied, sounding out the words after her, letter by letter, as she pointed."

The Lady turned to Abby. "Do you have a book with the things Dick learned to read?"

"Some of them," said the girl.

"Okay," said the Lady. "Bring it tomorrow."

She turned to Ben. "Look, it's not so bad. You're not stupid. Abby had a reading problem. She got over it. You will too.

"Now let's get the rest of Whittington's story before you go up to meet your granddad."

 **12**

# Dick Goes to London

THE CAT ROSE and settled on the railing like a blown leaf. He would have preferred to speak from his nest in the hay, but the Lady was of the firm opinion that audiences should look up. She said if folks looked down, they'd fall asleep. Where the cat perched, it was cold and drafty. A snowflake brushed his nose.

Whittington cleared his throat and hunched and settled, wrapping his ringed tail around his feet the way a gentleman wraps his scarf. He resumed in his rumbling, gravelly voice.

"One day, after the harvest, the land agent arrived. He came every few years in a carriage to inspect his master's properties and collect the rents. He was short, fat, and red-faced. His dark green coat buttoned tight over his belly.

"His driver was a quick, muscular man of thirty with a long scar down the side of his throat. His name was Will Price. He wore a tall black hat and a uniform patched with leather at the elbows, cuffs, and knees. His coat was black with green piping, but the piping had mostly worn off and the black was dulled with dust. His hair was lank and greasy, brown with gray in it.

"The boy asked Will if he and the agent were going to London.

"'Aye, in a roundabout way, collecting all that's due and righting all that's wrong,' said the driver. 'It'll be two months and more afore I see London again.'

"'May I go with you?' Dick asked.

"'Nay, lad. Many's the ones that's asked, though they've all been some older than you, but the agent would never have it. Besides, London's no place for a boy. . . .

"'For all of that, how old are you?'

"'Eight,' said Dick.

"Will was surprised. The boy had the manner of someone older but he looked about six. The driver muttered to himself that in this county, with food so poor, the children grew up runty.

"'Too young, lad. Try when you're fourteen and brawny.'"

Ben interrupted the cat's story. "I'm eight too. Am I bigger than he was?"

"Yes," said the cat.

"Hmm," said Ben.

The cat continued. "Dick offered to help on the road. He made every argument why Will should take him along.

'I know grooming, harness, tack, I can carry, keep the carriage nice, run errands. I can help dig it out and push in the miry places. I could spell you on the reins. I can sing.'

"Will just shook his head. He knew what the agent would say.

"When it was clear to the boy how it was, his face worked but he did not cry. It was a point of honor with him never to show tears.

"He made a plan. He put on all the clothes he owned and filched three loaves from the baker's rack. If he'd been caught, he would have been beaten, but he wasn't caught. He stuffed the loaves inside his shirt.

"Early the next morning as the carriage was pulling away, Dick jumped on the back and tangled himself in the luggage straps. He was scrawny but he was tough. Will couldn't dislodge him.

"'But your home! Your ma!' the driver pleaded, tugging at him.

"'I have to go to London,' the boy panted as he struggled to fix his grip tighter.

"The driver was not mean, but the agent was. When he saw a strange boy tangled in the straps on the back of his carriage, he was all for slashing at him with the horsewhip. He was too fat and out of breath to do it himself, so he screeched to his driver, 'Hit him, Will! Beat him! Whip the dirty beggar off.'

"Will wouldn't. He made up a story that Dick Whittington was a distant cousin and he was taking him to kin in London.

"'On your head and at your expense,' snarled the agent, clambering back into his carriage, red-faced and huffing.

"Long after they were out of sight of the village, Dick heard the single dry bell from his grandmother's church. He pictured her looking for him. His heart gave a jump. He blinked back tears.

"They were two months on the road. The roads were terrible, potted and dusty where they weren't puddled and clayey. In wet places the carriage would sink to its hubs in long ruts. Sometimes Dick walked ahead, scouting the driest way through a bog. When they got stuck, he dug and pushed alongside Will or went forward and pulled with the horses. He tried to please the grumpy man in the carriage. When the agent had to obey a call of nature, Dick brought the footstool and laid a path of brush over the mud.

"In some places there were overhanging branches and reports of thieves and highwaymen. Will kept beside him a long knife and a cloth sack of fist-sized stones. A few days after they'd left Dick's village, a wizened man lurched into the road waving a blade. The horses shied. As Will struggled to calm them, Dick fired a stone that hit the man in the thigh. The man squealed and stumbled backward into the brush. A week later and fifty miles on, in a remote place, two dirty-looking thugs rushed out from their hiding and grabbed the reins, pulling the horses into a swale. The horses reared. The carriage tipped. Will was roaring, trying to control the horses, when Dick put the knife in his teeth and dove under the flying straps. Balancing on the traces, he slashed at a hand. Its owner gaped as he sank under the flailing hoofs. Dick swung at the other man. The knife went deep. The reins went free.

"Will fought the pitching carriage back onto the highway and whipped the horses. It was rare that he struck them; usually a snap was enough for them to start or speed up. He hit now to settle them on running. There might be more robbers.

"Dick got cut deep from the corner of his mouth to his right ear when he pulled the knife from his teeth. When they rested the sweating horses, Will packed the boy's wound with a stinging plaster of cheese mold and moss that fell off only when the scab did. The cut itched but it never infected. For the rest of his life Dick carried a faint straight line across the right side of his face, not ugly but enough to notice.

"After that the agent paid for the boy's meals and for odd bits of clothing Will bought for him as they went along because it was getting cold. At every stop Will would ask if there was a boy Dick's size around and did his ma have shoes or trousers or a jacket she'd sell for little. Dick put on everything he got but there were never any shoes for him.

"'How did you get *your* scar?' the boy asked one drowsy afternoon as they lumbered along. Against Will's leathery throat the scar ran straight down like a piece of white cord.

"They were in open, rolling country now, with sheep grazing. The animals dotted the green mounds of grass and bracken like clots of cream. The old sheep looked on, motionless, as the carriage passed. The lambs frisked and gamboled like young rats. There was a constant music from the little ones. Will and Dick never saw a shepherd.

"'It was a halibut that done it,' Will said. 'I was choking and gagging and turning blue. Ma figured I was dead anyway, so she felt down my pipe to where things was stuck and cut it open to get the bone and all out. Then she stitched me up and here I be. There wasn't hardly any blood.'

"One evening Dick asked if he might polish the agent's boots. Old Radish Face allowed as he might and then allowed that he'd never had his boots come back so nice. Thereafter the boy got a mug of beer with his supper. A lot of vitamins in dark beer. He slept with the horses because it was fall now and they kept him warm."

"Beer?" Abby asked. "They gave him beer?"

"Everybody drank it then," the cat replied. "Beer or cider—what you'd call hard cider. It was safer than the water. He drank milk too when he could get it, but milk doesn't keep and cider does."

The cat continued. "Dick and Will talked and sang together through the long, slow days on the road. The boy came to trust the coachman. Will began to think of him as a younger brother. Dick told Will about his dream, and what he'd heard the carter say. He told his story with the fierceness of an old prophet, his lean face drawn and determined.

"'Those roads in London,' Will mused one afternoon, 'they be as hard as roads anywhere. . . .'

"Dick shook his head.

"'I'm going to London,' he said.

"'Ah, you've set your teeth and you're not to get shook loose. Like as not you'll end up lord mayor, but it will be a hard way. . . .' Will paused and looked at the grim-faced boy. Dick was staring down.

"'There's nothing to go back to,' he said quietly."

# 13

# Dick Arrives in London

"SLOWLY THEY CREPT UP on London and London crept up on them. First the market gardens, then the smoky outskirts with dumps and stockyards and slaughterhouses, tanneries, fat renderers, rag-and-bone places, smelters—all the dirty work of a city that the nicer sort of people who live there want to keep out of sight and never smell.

"London proper, when they finally got into it, was dark and cold. At London Bridge Dick swung off the carriage with a handshake for Will and a nod to the radish-faced agent. Radish Face gave him a grudging wave and flipped him a penny.

"By the time he'd left the carriage Dick knew it wasn't true about the streets of gold. It couldn't be—all those hungry-looking people around. Maybe he had to get away from the river to find the London he'd heard about at home. He walked the London streets for three days and never got away from the river and never found so much as a half-penny. He found people poorer than those he'd left at home. Once he'd spent his penny he begged for food and got kicked for his pains. He nearly starved to death.

"One evening he fainted in a doorway he was drawn to by the delicious smell of roasting meat. When he knocked at the door, the cook took her broom to him. He moaned and fainted. In a fury she hit him with the stick end, but he couldn't stand up. She was shoving his limp body toward the gutter when the merchant whose home it was arrived. He carried the boy inside.

"By the time Dick slumped down in the merchant's doorway his clothes were so worn and filthy they weren't worth washing. The cook was sent to borrow an outfit from a surprised neighbor who'd watched her give the broom to that very boy not an hour before."

Suddenly the cat stopped speaking. A rat had crept out after a bit of grain. The Lady didn't see it but the cat did. He tensed, his tail trembling. The Lady noticed his tail and guessed what was up.

"Wait, Whittington!" she yelled.

As the rat dove under a board, the cat drooped like a pitcher called from the mound.

"You, rat, come back out here," the Lady said. "You too, Old One. All of you. We're going to have a parley. For the moment you're safe under my protection."

The cat glowered as rats crept out of their holes and hiding spots around the barn. They gathered at the far edge of the stable, milling and chittering together, all eyes on Whittington.

The Lady flapped up on a hay bale. The chickens huddled together behind the cat, muttering and watching the rats.

"Quiet!" ordered the Lady. She turned to the rats. "You know what Whittington can do. He's the law now. If things don't change, sooner or later he'll get all of you.

Or we'll figure out a way to get along together. We don't want you taking our grain until we've first had our share. We don't want you going after our chicks and eggs anymore.

"That's what we want. What do you want in exchange?"

The Old One spoke. "To be safe from the cat."

There was a loud murmur from the rats behind him. "And a share of the grain," he added. "Especially in winter, when we can't get out."

The Lady looked at the chickens. "Are those terms okay?"

Nobody said anything.

"Yes," said the Lady.

She turned to the cat. "Whittington, you're the law, but I'm in charge. I say if the rats keep their word, we will keep ours. We'll leave them a share of what Bernie puts down and you won't go after them anymore. There's a lot of play in rats. It would be dull around here without their shows and parties. You'll see."

There was a faint cheer from the huddle of rats. The bantams and Coraggio hummed their surprise.

"Who knows," the Lady continued, "maybe someday the rats will be able to do something for you, like in the fable."

The cat looked up sulkily. "What's a fable?"

"A story that tells a truth," she said. "One day a nearsighted rat stumbled over the muzzle of a sleeping lion. His fur tickled the lion's nose and made him sneeze. The lion clumped his paw down on the rat.

"'Please,' gasped the rat. 'I'm sorry. Perhaps if you let me go, I'll live to perform some service for you in the future.'

"'Audacity and presumption!' snorted the lion. But then he smiled at the idea and lifted his paw. The rat limped off.

"A year later the lion got trapped in a hunter's net. It was a strong net, skillfully set. The lion lunged and clawed at the sinews that held him. It held tight. He roared for help. His friends came. Some tried digging under it, some tried pulling the net apart. No one could help him.

"The rat came. He knew what to do. He gnawed the cords with his sharp incisors and set the lion free.

"'Thank you,' said the lion, shaking himself tidy.

"'Tit for tat,' said the rat."

# 14

## Dick Is Given a Home

SCHOOL WAS CLOSED AGAIN because of snow. Ben was glad; it was a day like Saturday or Sunday, when he didn't have the tightness in his throat about having to read. They couldn't get the truck in, so Bernie and the kids pushed their way down to the barn with jugs of steaming water on the round sled.

After skidding the water down, the kids dragged the sled back up and whizzed down, twisting and balancing to take the curve, dragging arms and legs to hold down their speed. They did it a couple of times, shrieking and laughing so hard Bernie came out to watch. "My turn!" he yelled.

He hauled the sled up the hill, sat down, and was off before he was ready, arms and legs akimbo as the dish spun around and shot him down head first. The sled flipped on the curve and dumped him. The kids rushed to help. He got up slow, wiping snow from his face and hair, out from around his neck. He groped for his hat and tried to laugh. It hurt. The cigar was ruined.

It was cold and blowing, the way it gets right after a snow. When it's falling, the sky glows and the air warms up and takes on a spice smell. Once the front has passed, the air clears and the temperature drops. It was bitter that morning. The sky was blue with white streaks. Sounds carried in the cold, dry air. A jay soared, blue on blue. His call sounded like struck metal.

"Did you bring the book?" the Lady asked Abby as soon as Bernie was on his way back up the hill.

Abby had her Sunday-school book. It wasn't the Bible but it had psalms and parables.

"First Whittington's story," Ben said. The afternoon before he'd taken a kitchen knife and locked himself in the bathroom. He'd put the knife between his teeth and looked in the mirror. It looked better edge in. He got a small cut at the corner of his mouth. That night he'd dreamed that he was on the road to London with Will and the agent. He had become that scrawny boy in his imagining, deciding on his life.

The Lady agreed they could hear the rest of Whittington's story before they learned to read. She figured learning to read and the rest of Whittington's story could be done in a morning.

Whittington floated up to his place the way cats jump. He was looking sleeker. Maybe it was the diet of tuna and canned milk. Because it was blowing cold, the Lady had the kids pull down extra hay and ordered everyone to lie close together. It took a while to get settled because the chickens snuggling down tickled the horses, and the horses, without meaning to, shuddered the way they do to drive off flies, which sent the chickens flying. While all this was going on, the rats drew close and entertained themselves playing chase-my-tail and leapfrog, the next largest over the littlest and so on up to the Old One, who did not jump or chase his tail but sat rocking on his haunches waiting for the story.

"Once the merchant had the boy fed, washed, and clothed," the cat began, "he sat down with Dick and asked him what he could do.

"'Help around.'

"'Anyone can help around,' the old man said, not unkindly. 'What can you do that's special?'

"Dick didn't know. He had no skill, no trade; all he owned was his name. He told how he'd begun to learn to read and write. He said he could do small sums.

"'What work did you do at home?' the merchant asked.

"'Simpling for my grandmother. She concocted.'

"'You know plants?'

"'Some.'

"The merchant pressed his thumb against his nose

and nodded. That was his way of tucking away something important.

"'Teach me what needs doing,' the boy said. 'I'll do it.'

"He had spirit. He wasn't sorry for himself. He would ask but he wouldn't whine.

"The merchant's name was Hugh Fitzwarren. His cook was a small-eyed woman, squat, round-faced, gap-toothed. She wore layers and layers of tops and skirts and kept an iron pan tied to her belt for protection in the streets. She was as much family as Fitzwarren had. She was not a good cook and she had a dark temper, but the merchant felt responsible for her. And now he had this boy on his hands.

"Dick tried to stay awake to argue how he could be useful to the merchant and his cook, but fatigue and a full stomach overwhelmed him. His head sagged. He fell asleep on the table. Fitzwarren carried him to his own bed.

"He summoned his cook for a talk. She was told to feed the boy back to strength. He gave her money to buy him clothes. He added that she might scold but she was never again to beat him. If the boy was so bad as to deserve beating, Fitzwarren said he'd turn him out. But he was not to be hit. The merchant was against all beating and flogging, although most children were beaten in his time.

"Fitzwarren was comfortable, not rich. He was a cloth merchant. He wore the livery of his guild, a long velvet coat the deep green color of sea moss."

"What's a guild?" Abby asked.

"A group of merchants chartered to carry on a particular business. No one but a guild member could practice that trade. The guild set standards of quality. Fitzwarren was a member of the Mercers Company. Mercers dealt in cloth and fabric.

"He imported small quantities of precious fabrics and sold English woolens abroad. Wool was the great product of England then, raw and woven. England's wools were the standard of the world. Her fortunes depended on it. Even so, English people of quality liked to flaunt fine silks, brocades and satins, glowing velvets, flashing taffetas. The gentry were the merchant's principal customers.

"Fitzwarren's shop smelled of new wool and spices. Along with fabrics, as agent for a friend who was a member of the Pepperers and Spicers Guild, he did a small, steady business in remainders of spice shipments he was offered by ship captains when he was on the docks seeing to his other cargoes. He bought pepper, cinnamon, cloves, nutmegs, and cardamoms, along with pure white rock salt mined in Germany.

"For pleasure, Fitzwarren bought the strange roots, slips, seeds, bulbs, and plants that captains, mates, and sailors sometimes had for sale on their return from foreign lands. He was always handy with money in his pocket when a ship docked.

"He gardened for flowers and sweet smells. He had exotics in his garden—clove-smelling gillyflowers; peaches he raised against the wall from pits carried up the Silk Road from China by the traders; tulips from Turkey; daffodils; salad greens grown under glass for his table year-round. Few ate salads in his time.

"He had a bush from the Orient whose berries were said to make goats drunk, and a scarlet French strawberry with gold dots like the queen's robe. There were things in his beds that never came to flower because the London sun didn't burn long and hot enough.

"His garden was strange-looking, the plants tucked helter-skelter in long raised beds edged with cow shins and knucklebones. Violets, periwinkles, and tiny hyacinths carpeted the narrow paths. He might have made things handsome and patterned like his neighbors' had he ever stood back and looked at it all as a garden. He never did. He was always hunched over one plant or another.

"One evening in the garden Fitzwarren asked Dick if he recognized any of the plants.

"'Oh yes sir, the celandine there for sore throat when boiled with wine. The catmint my grandmother would honey the young tops into a conserve for nightmare. The green hellebore she concocted into a potion for worming children. . . .'

"Again Fitzwarren pressed his thumb against his nose."

**15**

# The Boy Goes to Work for Fitzwarren

"SINCE HIS BUSINESS had to do with consignments and cargoes in many ships, Fitzwarren spent part of every day hurrying around the docks, delivering and collecting his packages and keeping an eye out for sailors who had plants and strange things to sell. You had to be quick to survive there, and tough. The docks were no place for the timid.

"The merchant was getting on. Fifty-odd was a high age then. The boy appeared quick and tough even though he was half starved. He could read and figure enough to manage the waybills. He was anything but timid. Fitzwarren decided to try Dick on the docks. He could handle the smaller parcels and keep a watch for curiosities. He knew something about plants.

"The boy started going down to the water with Fitzwarren to collect consignments. He studied how the merchant jollied the captains as he paid them so his dealings always seemed more pleasure than business. He paid attention to how his master arranged for cartage of the bigger loads to his countinghouse and how he dickered with the sailors for bulbs, roots, nuts, odd carvings, beads, weavings, shrunken heads, mermaid hands. They bought all those things.

"The boy's pay was such clothing as the cook turned up, room in the merchant's drafty attic, his board. Breakfast was milk warm from the cow, porridge, and dark bread with butter. Dinner—what we call lunch—was hard-boiled eggs or a cold roast chicken he shared with Fitzwarren and washed down with bitter ale. For supper, roast meat of some kind, greens from Fitzwarren's garden, a piece of fruit, bread, and cider. Sometimes there was a suet pudding if the cook was in good humor. The pudding was rich but it wasn't sweet. Sugar was something rare.

"It wasn't long before Dick was on the docks alone with money to pay for the orders and something extra in case he saw a curiosity. He made the docks his own, recognizing the regulars, learning their names and trades. He got to know the wherrymen and porters, the loiterers, the ones to keep away from.

"He would jump into the small boats that ran from the docks to meet the ships before they docked. He'd haul himself up the ropes like a sailor to vault onto the deck. He learned the merchant's eye for rarities and his smiling skill at bargaining. Sometimes Dick had to pay with a promise. Word soon got around that if you sold him on credit, he was sure to be back early with what he owed. That word always gets around.

"Within a year he was more the size of boys his age. The cook took pride in that. Her meals had got better with someone hungry to cook for. Her temper had sweetened too; she smiled sometimes. She was beautiful when she smiled. Dick managed now and then to bring her a bead that had come by land and sea from India, a bright bit of Africa cloth he'd got from one of the sailors.

"London was a town of ocean fogs coming in with the smells of the river, sea moss, fish, old rope, decaying hulls, salt, smoke, hints of cooking. Bells sounded the hours, calls to worship, alarms, laments for the dead. Dick got up to the first tinkling ones. Then the large ones started. There was no pattern to the bells' ringing, the deep ones galloping along, the smaller, high-pitched ones going as fast as they could like small dogs racing around big ones. Most of the London bells had more silver in them than the bell in his grandmother's church at home. That one had made a harsh, dry clank. The few times he heard one in London that sounded like it he'd see his grandmother's face and his knees would go weak with homesickness. He was nine years old.

"This is where the cat comes in. . . ."

"I was wondering about the cat," said the Lady. "But now it's time for the reading lesson."

# 16

# Ben's First Reading Lesson in the Barn

WHITTINGTON SAID BEN should sit close beside Abby because that was the way Dick had done with his grandmother. Abby was to read very slowly, pointing with her finger at each letter as she sounded it out, and then repeat the word as the old lady had done. Then Ben would read it aloud, sounding out the same way Dick had.

They started with a psalm.

Whittington said Ben should learn that word first, so Abby had him sound it out letter by letter. He could make all the sounds okay.

"P-s-a-l-m."

The *p* was a problem. Abby explained that sometimes letters in words are silent, like the *p* in "psalm" and the *s* in "island." Everyone looked blank.

"What does 'psalm' look like?" Whittington asked. He'd seen words before but they'd never interested him. Now, watching Ben struggle with this word, he wanted to see it.

Abby tried to show him in the book but the cat got lost in the sea of marks on the page.

She fished a pencil from her backpack and drew the word in big capital letters across the nearest stanchion—"PSALM."

They all stared up at it—children, chickens, duck, cat, horses. The rats had gathered too, rocking on their haunches, whispering to each other nose to nose in their way. The animals gathered around like the devout witnessing a miracle. It *was* a miracle. Out of five black marks that had their origins a thousand generations back in a place lost to memory, Ben conjured up sounds that made a word that in turn evoked the presence of something that wasn't there. He got the picture of "psalm" and how it should sound, and he locked it away forever. But he always had to be careful to skip the tricky *p* that started it.

"So now you have one word already," said the cat, who had no idea how many words there were but realized it was going to take more than a morning to get this boy reading half as well as his sister.

"'The Lord is my shepherd . . . ,'" Abby read, sounding out each letter and pointing as she went.

"'The Lord is my . . . shhh . . . ,'" Ben repeated.

"'He maketh me to lie down in green pastures. . . .'"

"'He maketh me to lie b-b-b-b . . .'"

"No," said the girl, "*d,* not *b.*"

This went on for a while. When they finally got to the fourth verse and Ben read "beath" for "death," it was as Whittington remembered and just as painful.

"You're reversing," he said. "That's what my boy did—the boy in my home before. They said he read *b*'s for *d*'s, *d*'s for *b*'s, *p*'s for *q*'s, *a*'s for *e*'s. They called it dyslexia, which didn't tell him anything. Before he was sent away his parents were giving him lists of words to memorize so he'd know that since there's no such thing as 'beath,' the word has to be 'death.'"

The cat didn't tell how furious his boy's parents got when he missed, how their anger added to the child's confusion.

"Maybe you could do what he did—memorize a list of words every week." The cat figured Abby wouldn't pressure Ben the way his first boy's parents had.

Ben looked dubious.

The Lady was dismayed. She'd learned to swim in less time than it took this boy to do a Bible verse. She wondered if it was worth the effort. Animals had gotten along without reading for a long time.

That night, when he came over to tuck in the animals, Bernie's flashlight picked up "PSALM" written across the stanchion. He wondered for a moment, but his knee hurt and the water jug was leaking.

# 17

## Blackie Arrives

IT GOT DOWN TO ten degrees below zero that night. The next morning a man in town who kept chickens went out and found his black hen frozen. Somehow she'd got out of the henhouse and became stuck in the snow. He revived her in cool water, everything except her feet. They were wrecked. She'd be too much trouble for him now, but how do you throw out a lame hen? Bernie was the only person he knew who would keep her. On his way to the Texaco he stopped and bought two cigars. Bernie was out on a road test when the man with the hen got to the station. He left her in a milk crate with a note and the cigars and drove off with an easy conscience.

Bernie swore when he saw the hen and the cigars. Even without reading the note he knew why she was there. She didn't seem to be suffering, though. She was cheerful, clucking and excited about everything; she just couldn't work her feet. She hobbled and flutter-jumped to get around. She didn't fall over. Bernie pocketed the cigars and drove her out to the barn.

A while back the grandkids had kept rabbits. He'd built a hutch for them on an old table. The rats had done in the rabbits. The hutch was in the back of the barn somewhere among the abandoned cars, old gas pumps, skis, and everything else that gets tucked away in a barn. Bernie dragged it out and brushed it off, made a bed of hay in it, and cut down a milk carton for a water dish. He put the hen in the hutch with a cleaned-out tuna can of the sweet molasses grain. She flapped and staggered around in her new quarters, found the grain and water, and settled in.

The animals watched all of this with interest. No sooner had Bernie headed back up the hill than Coraggio clambered up on the hutch and the two chickens started burbling away at each other, the cockerel telling his story, Blackie the hen telling hers. They became such friends Bernie had to cut a hole in the top of the hutch so Coraggio could sleep next to her. They churred softly together for hours every day, heads close like people whispering secrets.

Outside, everything was covered in white except the mound of horse manure and spent hay Bernie added to every afternoon. The heat from the rot going on in that pile kept it warm for earthworms, grubs, maggots, insect eggs, and small animals like mice, voles, and moles. The mound steamed across winter like a dark freighter.

# 18

## Dick Meets His Cat

THE NEXT DAY after school, Abby brought her word-book. She read aloud the first list, *ei* and *ie* words—"receive" to "grieve." Whittington said those were too hard. The Lady said twelve were too many. With Abby reading, the choices they ended up with were "coming," "hoping," "weigh," "foreign," and "writing." Abby wrote out the words in block letters and taped the list on the stanchion under "PSALM."

"Coming" and "hoping" went pretty well after some to-and-fro about the different sounds of *o*. It was a relief that *ing* always sounded the same. Ben got stuck on "weigh." "Why does it have *ig* in it? It doesn't make sense!" Ben snapped. "I can say the letters in it okay, I just can't make the word sound out. That's what gets me in trouble in school, silent letters. You never know which ones not to say."

Abby admitted she couldn't make "weigh" work either if she sounded out every letter. Ben jumped up and drew an angry line through it. Everyone was tense.

"Stretch! Time to stretch!" the Lady yelled with a great flap. Coraggio had been holding his breath through "weigh." Now he uttered a powerful crow. The horses and the kids headed out for a dash around. The bantams bickered furiously until the Lady hushed them.

She looked at the cat. His mouth was pulled tight. Ben's bewilderment reminded him of the boy in his home before. He didn't want Ben to suffer and be sent away like that boy.

When Abby and Ben came back in, the cat made them sit down together for a minute and take deep breaths. "We all fell down learning to walk," he said. "We don't remember how hard it was or how much it hurt. Once Dick learned to read he blotted out how his grandmother had thwacked him with a switch when he missed something she thought he should know. It was what the priest had done to her. He said the pain would help her remember the next time. 'Make it sound alive,' his grandmother would say with a swat. 'Give it life, louder, like you're sure of it.'

"Now, back to the lesson."

"Writing" went no better. "What's the *w* for? It's tricking me!" Ben was wincing to keep back tears when the Lady ordered Whittington back up to his storytelling place on the rail.

The cat waited for the horses to come back in. He needed a moment to gather himself. He was shaking.

"Dick had been with Fitzwarren for almost two years. He was ten. He'd grown. He'd learned something of the mercer's trade.

"On New Year's Day Fitzwarren gave Dick a half-penny. It doesn't sound like much but it was a valuable sum then.

"As Dick walked to the docks, he fingered the coin in his pocket and wondered what he should buy. Suddenly he saw my great-great-grandmother's grand-mother, thirty generations back.

"The strange cat eyed him in a knowing way and nodded.

"Dick knew he had to have that cat. He'd thought about getting a cat to check the mice and rats that skittered in his room at night and gnawed his things. He knew the cook wouldn't allow it.

"There was something arresting about the way this cat engaged eyes. Most animals won't lock eyes with men. Goats do, and snakes, which is why we associate them with evil. The rest of us look away in shame or embarrassment when someone looks us in the eye. But this was different, this was a stare of recognition, the way you can't take your eyes off someone you're eager to see: you want to embrace them with your eyes.

"Dick's hair went up. He knocked on the door behind where the cat was sitting.

"Silence. He knocked again. Nothing. Again he knocked. At last there was a shuffling and the door opened a little and then a little more, as if whoever was opening it was having a hard time getting used to the light.

"Finally there stood before Dick an ancient bald man in a long velvet coat the deep green color of sea moss. His brown fur collar was turned up. The man said nothing, he just looked at the boy. He was slight, his skin was milk white and almost transparent, wrinkled like tissue paper. His eyes were small and blue, red-rimmed, piercing. At first he seemed to recognize Dick. In the next instant it was as if he were staring through him.

"'S-sir,' stammered the boy, 'will you please sell me your cat?'

"The man looked down at the cat as if he'd never seen her before. Then he looked back at Dick and studied him from head to toe. Finally he asked in a high old man's voice how much money he had.

"'Ha'penny, sir.'

"The man nodded and held out his hand. His hand was thin, he had long fingers.

"Dick dug for his coin and laid it in the man's palm.

The palm was warm and dry. The long fingers closed slowly around the coin and the man slipped back inside.

"Dick didn't have to pick up his cat or lead her away on a string. The cat followed him as if they'd always walked together. When they got home, he tried to sneak her to his room. The cook caught him. She always knew everything.

"'What have you there?' she asked, smacking his shirt. The cat heaved out and shot up the stairs.

"'Nay!' she bellowed. 'Nay to nitbags, nay to pets!'

"She snatched her broom and took after the cat like she'd swatted at Dick that first evening. The stairs up to the attic were narrow. Dick's room was low and tight. Wheezing and out of breath, she took a swipe here and a swipe there. Her broom never met the cat. It was like she was fanning a butterfly that, almost without her seeing, sailed downstairs and disappeared. 'I'll . . . I'll have it out with your master, I will,' she stormed.

"She never did. She softened toward the cat when it presented the rat that had been spoiling the potatoes.

"That evening Fitzwarren came home with a ship captain who shared the merchant's passion for rare plants. Fitzwarren's best knuckleboned bed was set aside for things the captain had brought him. In the last light the two men looked carefully at a thick shoot sprouting

from a large nut found floating off the African coast. A few yards on there was a collection of aromatics— peppermint, catmint, lavenders, sages.

"There was a gravel bed of thymes—some rough, some woolly, large-leaved and small, from France, Spain, and Greece. You picked up their scent if you so much as brushed them. The bees loved those plants.

"Beyond, against a wall, was a row of grafted fruit trees the captain had brought Fitzwarren over the years. Dessert that night was compote of fruits from those trees: peaches, pears, and cherries in honeyed brandy. The cherries colored the syrup dark red.

"Back inside the two men talked, heads close together. As the punch bowl emptied and filled, the captain's tongue loosened and he told Fitzwarren about a powerful herb to be found on the Barbary Coast. The herb was said to melt painful stones of the kidney and bladder, a great affliction in those times and now.

"The captain couldn't tell his friend more about this precious herb because he'd been sworn to secrecy by the king who'd told him about it. It was the king's dream to harvest this plant and make a fortune for his people, the way the ancient Phoenician princes at Tyre had profited from the secret of the purple dye they got from the shellfish *Murex*.

"The captain had just finished speaking when the cat came in with a plump brown rat. She laid it at the captain's feet.

"Fitzwarren was embarrassed. He'd already scolded Dick about wasting his money on a pet; now this disgrace. The captain was delighted.

"'What a fine cat! In London you're never more

than six feet from a rat. It's even closer on shipboard. They foul our food, they make stinks. Why, if I had this cat with me aboard the *Unicorn* . . .'

"The captain took Dick Whittington's cat on his lap. As he stroked her, he told her about the herb, *Amapacherie,* that would melt painful stones. He'd sworn to tell no man his secret, but he could tell the cat, and if the merchant and his boy happened to overhear, well, so much for that.

"Fitzwarren and the captain talked long into the night. The cat stayed snug in the captain's lap and purred and purred—a most singular, deep, and musical purr.

"That night it was arranged that Dick and his cat would sail for the Barbary Coast on the *Unicorn* and see to the buying of a cargo for Fitzwarren. Dick was to keep a sharp eye for plants. Fitzwarren gave him a purse, some sheets of stiffened cloth to press the leaves and flowers of plants he found, a few small cloth sacks for seeds and bulbs.

"Fitzwarren came down to Limehouse Wharf to see them off. As Dick got ready to jump into the wherry that would carry him to the ship, Fitzwarren put out his hand, then started to wrap the boy in a hug. He caught himself and turned away.

"The cat jumped into the wherry on her own."

# 19

## Out with the Owls

BERNIE BROUGHT Ben and Abby along one night when he came to tuck in the animals. It was clear and cold, no moon. The air was still. The kids were curious about where the cat slept, but he wasn't sleeping. He was jumpy. He waited until Bernie was busy with the jugs.

"Ben," he whispered, "can you whistle?"

"Sure."

"Good. Let's sneak out to the pond and whistle for owls. They're claiming territory now. You can hear them. If you can whistle like they do, they'll come. Get Abby. I'll get the others."

The rooster wouldn't go. Without him the bantams wouldn't go either. The horses couldn't go and neither could Blackie, so it was a small crowd that crunched to the far end of the frozen-over pond. The Lady had never been out so late. The cat had to guide her, she couldn't see anything. Something told her it wasn't a good idea for a duck to be out calling owls at night, but Whittington insisted. Ben held Abby's hand hard.

"When I was little and scared of the dark, Mom told me it's never absolutely black out," Abby said. "Once your eyes adjust it's blue velvet because of the stars. Look up—it's like somebody threw glitter." They stopped and looked.

"Anyway," Abby continued, "even if you can't see, you can sense things like trees and stones in your way."

The Lady couldn't. Ben couldn't either. As they bumped and stumbled along, the Lady asked Whittington, "How can you see where you're going?"

"I'm nocturnal," he answered.

The Lady was too proud to ask what "nocturnal" meant. It always annoyed her when Whittington used big words. She'd had a brother who was a smarty like that. Alas, he got taken by the hawk. As soon as she remembered that, she forgave Whittington.

The cat sensed her annoyance. "It means I'm a night creature," he said.

Then they could all see. The pond loomed like an opal. It seemed to float in its own light above the land around it. They could see the puffs their breaths made.

The owls were out. You could hear them. Ben picked up their call. When the cat nudged him and whispered, "Whistle!" Ben gave a low, fluttering call that drifted down in tone like the owls' love song. "Again!" Whittington said. Ben whistled again.

They heard something. A few seconds later there was a rush of wind overhead, then a screech of rage as the owl Ben had called discovered the trick. In his surprise, the owl dropped the kill he'd been carrying to his mate. Something soft and furry hit Ben's shoulder and thumped to the ground. Ben shrieked. They all ran away as fast as they could.

"What were you doing?" Bernie asked as they stumbled back into the barn. The kids were bright-cheeked and out of breath. Whittington was fluffed up, like when he'd fought Havey. The Lady had flap-dashed all the way back; it would take her a while to settle her feathers.

Bernie was loading the jugs on the sled. He didn't wait for an answer.

He let the kids go out before him, then he pushed the door to and slid in place the board that held it shut. Anyone who wanted to could get in, but this was Bernie's way of locking up.

As Bernie and the kids stumped up the hill, the Lady settled into her nest of hay and feathers by the door. The cat lay down close beside her. The rats came out to dance, squeaking, leaping, mock-boxing, chasing tails, rolling over each other in somersaults and flips, all to their own music. It happened every night after Bernie left. As suddenly as it had begun, their dance ended and they went their separate ways to hunt for food.

When they came back, the rats rolled up together in a warm ball in their underground sleeping parlor.

The Lady turned her head almost completely around and tucked her bill under her wing. The chickens did the same with their beaks. Whittington's nose was under his paws, one folded over the other. The horses closed their eyes. Soon the only sounds in the barn were breathing and an occasional snort when one of the horses blew out a hay tickle.

## 20

# Spooker Is Sick

ONE MORNING the kids and Bernie noticed that Spooker didn't frisk around the paddock to greet them when they arrived. She pawed the ground. More alarming, she didn't eat. At noon, when Bernie went back with Havey, Spooker was lying on her side, rolling and groaning. Havey went over, sniffed her thoughtfully, and investigated her droppings. The dog took a scientific interest in illness. If a chicken was sick, Havey nosed it like a medic. A dead one she'd stand over soberly, like a paid mourner.

Bernie called the vet. The vet told him to get Spooker back on her feet and keep her walking until she could get there.

"Colic," the vet said. "Cramps. She's rolling to get the pain out. Get her walking or she'll get her stomach all twisted up and then there's no saving her."

Bernie tried to get her up but he couldn't. He called Al and Wayne, the mechanic, to come out from the Texaco. They shut down the station and rushed over to save the horse.

Al brought along the hand winch they used to move cars. It had a broad belt at one end and a hook at the other. He fixed the hook to a stanchion and worked the belt under the horse.

The three men cranked the winch and got Spooker up. She groaned deeply with every breath and kept trying to lie down again. She wasn't interested in walking. Havey sat and watched. She'd never shown such interest in the horse before.

The vet's ambulance was a red pickup with heavy tires, stainless steel lockers and drawers built into the sides, a sterilizer, drums of water and medicine, pumps, hoses, and a small crane at the back. There were spotlights front and back so she could work out in a field if necessary. She could drive it anywhere. She had big, strong hands, sure hands. She spoke to Spooker with her hands.

The vet closed her eyes and put her ear to the horse's side, then to her belly.

"Colic."

She looked in Spooker's mouth.

"Teeth need filing."

"Uh-oh," Bernie said. "The man who shoes 'em called a while back to set it up. I forgot."

"Horse teeth are too important to forget," the vet said. "It's not like your forgetting to floss. I'll explain why in a minute."

From one of the truck lockers she took a container of castor oil and a small pump with a hose. She added calming medicine to the oil and stuck the hose into the horse's mouth. The vet pumped; the horse gagged. Spooker tried to back away but the stuff went down.

They tied her head to the stanchion. The vet got out a thick, stubby rasp. With Bernie and the others cooing at the wide-eyed horse, the vet pried open Spooker's jaws, locked them open with a chock of wood, and proceeded to file the edges of her teeth to make them sharp.

"She's worn the edges off, so she's not chewing fine enough," the vet explained. "What she's swallowing is too big to pass through. The mass gets jammed in her gut, it ferments, gas builds up and cramps her. Another few hours, it would have taken operating to save her."

Bernie said he'd seen that operation on *60 Minutes*.

"They cut open that horse," he said, "took out yards and yards of gut, found the blockage, cut that out, sewed up the pipe, stuffed the guts back inside that horse every which way, sewed her up again.

"And you know, she lived!

"What was it that you added to the oil?"

"The narcotic? It's for her cramps. Codeine and something like Pepto-Bismol. She'll doze on that all day and most of tomorrow. If I'd given you that dose, you'd be off playing harps."

As the vet packed her kit, she said, "Watch her poops. She's going to go a lot the next day or two because of the castor oil, then she'll taper off to what she's supposed to do regular, which is four or five a day. It's like my Italian grandma said, 'Clear bowels, a merry heart.'"

Bernie kept Spooker strapped so she couldn't lie down. She was in dreamland for the better part of two days, doing everything the vet said she would do. In her professional capacity, Havey studied every evidence of that horse. Then Spooker was better and very hungry and forgot how they'd tied her up and purged her and made her mouth hurt. Forgetting is forgiving.

# 21

## Ben's Reading

THE SUN WAS GAINING on winter. There was a new smell in the air. The pond boomed and cracked as the ice broke up. In the paddock bare places appeared with puddles of meltwater the Lady found pleasant for bathing. There were robins and the *scree* of red-winged blackbirds claiming territory still under snow. Around the pond margin, celandines made tiny suns and skunk cabbages bloomed squat, plum-colored cowls streaked with gold. They were rank-smelling. Nobody ate them. Winter rye in the fields was going from yellow to green as it unrumpled. With the finches it was all the other way. Bernie counted spring from when the finches started going from dirty green to yellow.

The road was grease again. Bernie had to hike down the hill. The pump had thawed free, though, so there was water handy. Coraggio and his band of bantams were parading out farther and farther every day after morsels, infuriating Marker, the dog who watched everything from the house on the hill.

The rooster was expert at kicking away straw and dung and finding knots of pink worms. When he turned those up, the bantams cheered as if they'd found candy. The Lady followed too, eager for new green shoots and the fat gray grubs Coraggio excavated. The bantams were back to laying eggs. Abby and Ben hunted for them. The rats were holding to the pact. There were occasional stinks from eggs the bantams forgot and the kids didn't find. The stink of a rotten egg is noble.

It worried Abby the way the chickens went after worms. In school Mrs. Harris told them that worms plow more soil than all the tractors in the world. Abby figured the way Coraggio and his gang were going after them, there wouldn't be any worms left.

Ben struggled with his half dozen words a day, trying not to guess, taking his time. They'd abandoned Abby's spelling book. The cat said those words were too advanced, they should concentrate on everyday words— words for things the boy could see, like "egg," "ice," "chicken," "barn," "horse." Ben did better with those. What worked best, though, were Dick's maxims, like "Tell Truth, and shame the Devil." Ben read that through once with Abby helping. The second time he got it on his own. He was tickled.

"But he's not reading," Abby said. "He memorized. He's reciting."

"So what?" said the cat. "That's the way Dick learned, reciting from memory as he followed the letters."

Abby wasn't sure that counted.

Whittington had some more of Dick's remember-ables for Abby to copy and tape up under "PSALM":

"A cat may look on a King."

"If you know not me, you know nobody."

"Time and tide wait for no man."

"What is no good for the bee is no good for the hive."

"And here's one by a dog about his dead master," Whittington added:

*Augustus Jones taught me to beg.*

*Upon his bones I lift my leg.*

Ben read them on his own the second time through. Abby was still dubious. "That's not going to help him with his book in school. And it isn't touching numbers. The worst is the numbers." Ben glowered; the cat's eyes narrowed.

"Enough!" the Lady said. "Time for the story."

## 22

# To Africa on the *Unicorn*

WHITTINGTON TOOK HIS PLACE.

"By the time the merchant saw Dick off at Lime-house Wharf, the boy had become more than his clerk. Fitzwarren gave him a square of blue silk to tie around his neck for luck. Dick was eleven. He knew which fabrics and spices would do well in the shop, how to judge their quality, how much to pay for them. Fitzwarren knew he would find good things and buy wisely. If the voyage went well, the shop would profit.

"The risk of it, though, was more than a merchant's risk for Fitzwarren. The boy had gained a place in his heart. Then, as now, the sea claimed many, what with storms, wars, pirates, and the risk of diseases like scurvy on board and plague in port."

"What's scurvy?" Ben asked.

"On long voyages without fresh fruits and vegetables the crew's gums began to bleed, they got bruises, and their joints went bad. We know now it's caused by lack of vitamin C."

"Gran gives us stuff with vitamin C," Abby said.

The cat nodded. "We make our own. Only humans have that problem.

"The ship Dick and his cat hauled away in was small and vulnerable," he continued. "Her mainsail had a strange green stripe across the top. The other sails in the harbor were tan, brown, and white. From her forward halyard she flew the flag of St. George, a red cross on a white field. It was a sign that the vessel was from a Christian country. From where Fitzwarren stood the ship looked tiny.

"The sea was bigger than anything Dick had ever seen, boring and endless until the wind moaned and slammed and it became hills and swoops of black oil he was sure would drown him as the ship heaved and shuddered worse than the agent's carriage when the robbers attacked it.

"Their trip took three weeks. The cat got her sea legs quickly. Dick was seasick for days. His bed was a shallow bunk. It was always moving. He wanted more than anything for his bed to hold still. The only light came from an oil lamp that guttered and shifted on its mounting near his head. The smoke didn't help how he felt.

Then one day he was well. He was never seasick again. He slept on deck no matter what the weather.

"The fresh food ran out and the water grew stale. They ate porridge, dried apples, salt fish and salt pork, peas, beans, cheese, pickled cabbage, and hardtack— small ingots of saltless bread baked hard and packed dry so it wouldn't rot. There were daily rations of hard cider. When their lines were lucky, they had fresh fish. Sometimes there were eggs from the chickens on board, sometimes a cup of goat's milk, once a dinner of roast goat.

"They sailed south down the coast of France, then across the Bay of Biscay to put in at Lisbon, where they got fresh water and traded for black peppercorns, wine, oil, and olives. The men they traded with served them cups of sweetened tea and dried figs. Dick's eyes widened as he tasted for the first time the fig's honey-like sweetness.

"From Lisbon they sailed into the Mediterranean, past Gibraltar, where only twelve miles of water separate Europe from Africa. Dick looked to his right and there was all of Africa in a red haze.

"On board, meanwhile, among ballast, stores, fetid water, and spilled cargo, the cat made a great slaughter of rats. It was her habit to lay the kills on deck by the hatchway. The sailors cheered as they flung the rats into the water by their tails."

There were moans from the dark part of the barn, where the rats were listening.

"The cat became the pet of everyone," Whittington continued.

"They landed at Tripoli in North Africa and called upon the king there, who was a particular friend of the captain's. It was he who had whispered the secret of *Amapacherie,* the healing herb he hoped to gain a fortune by.

"The boy squinted in the glare. Unlike London, where they build to catch the sun, here everything was built to avoid it. The palace entrance was pale yellow. There were greenish blue tiles with Arabic writing that spelled out 'Above All Things Is Justice.'

"The palace was a hodgepodge of low forts and shrines built around courtyards shaded with palm trees. The hard palm leaves clacked in the slight breeze. Dick had never seen a palm before.

"Inside, the palace was a labyrinth of dirty, narrow passages with slit windows. The passages led to small dark rooms—closets, storage chambers, and sleeping quarters for soldiers and court retainers. The only light came from the slit windows that let in a constant stream of dust and fine sand, insects and dried leaves. The passageways were paved with bricks. There were shallow stairs where you wouldn't expect them. A couple of times Dick stumbled in the gloom. The cat rode on his shoulder.

"In the room where Dick was sent to wash and relieve himself a large rat jumped from the cistern, frightening the cat. In her surprise, she clawed her master. She was embarrassed and vowed vengeance on that rat."

"What's a cistern?" Abby asked.

"A large water pot," Whittington replied.

"And the rat was in it?" Abby asked.

The cat nodded. Abby shuddered.

"The throne room was round and shadowed," he continued. "Fresh air and light came from an opening in the roof that directed a spot of brightness to one place. Very slowly the spot moved around the room. In the center the king sat, large and shapeless on a bed of embroidered silks. He held a wand of long feathers with rows of round gold-colored eyes said to spy out evil. They had been bright once. When he wanted something, he thumped his wand and four men jumped.

"Around the room were large and small cages with peacocks, parrots, parakeets, and other birds, all whooping and chattering. Rats and mice scurried about. It smelled of bird dirt and the perfumed smoke coming from a large bronze can with holes in its sides and top. A veiled woman in a white gown passed a plate of dates to the visitors. Dick had never eaten a date before. The fruit was sweet and grainy. When she passed the plate again, he took another.

"The king was more olive-colored than brown. His face was as smooth as a baby's, soft, hairless, slightly wrinkled except around his eyes and forehead. His hair was long, black, pulled back, and tied so tight his eyes bulged. The back of his hand, when Dick bent to kiss it, was cold and sticky like a frog's back. He was a great warrior. The birds had been given to him as tribute.

"As the captain and the king talked, their murmuring and the steady bird racket made Dick sleepy. The cat was resting in his lap. Suddenly she stiffened, tensed, and soared across the room to land on a rat. The battle was brief. She knew exactly where to bite at the back of the neck to sever the spinal cord.

"The king heard the rat's death shriek. Rats ruled his palace; his kingdom was infested with vermin. When he heard how Dick Whittington's cat had cleared the *Unicorn* of rats, he swore he had to have her, whatever the cost. At that moment she deposited the dead rat at his feet. There was no ratter like her in his kingdom.

"He was rich and impatient. He was used to getting his way. He did not like to bargain because that put him on equal footing with another person. Since he was superior to everyone, his way of dealing was to take by force when he could and in every other circumstance to offer such an overwhelming price the trade was settled immediately.

"In exchange for the cat, he offered the cargo Dick had selected from his warehouses—bales of raw cotton from the desert countries, bundles of woven silk that had come overland from China and India, dyestuffs, rare gums, wrapped blocks of opium, casks of wine and oil, circles of pressed figs, cakes of precious sugar, sacks of cardamom, ginger, cinnamon, cloves.

"Dick was astonished. The cat was more than his friend. He had more feeling for her than for anyone. Yet she was looking up at him with the strange knowing look she'd given him the first time he'd seen her in front of Greencoat's. Her look said 'okay' and suggested he keep silent. He couldn't speak anyway; he could hardly breathe.

"The king was so anxious to buy the cat, he took the boy's silence for a merchant's shrewdness to get a better price.

"With a slap of his fat hands and an angry squeal, he ordered his first man to bring a bag of jewels. Dick was too bewildered to say anything. The captain was kicking him and muttering. The cat sat in Dick's lap looking on and purring loudly.

"Suddenly she vanished.

"'So, my young master,' said the king, nodding and screwing his mouth into a smile he didn't feel and holding up his hands in pretend surrender. 'What may I add to the cargo and the jewels?'

"'The *Amapacherie*,' whispered Dick.

"The king gasped. 'How did you know . . . ?'

"At that moment, another rat screamed its last.

"'Yes,' the king murmured, 'for to have such a cat would be a boon to my people. They would be able to save their food, and their homes would be cleaner. She will bear generations of ratters.'

"Dick exchanged the cat for the cargo, the jewels, and sacks of the herb and its seeds. He had the same lost feeling he'd had when he heard the harsh, dry bell of home. It felt wrong to let the cat go, even though she'd given him a signal. There was no parting. The cat had disappeared before the boy could change his mind.

"'All will be well,' said the captain. 'Back in London you'll find another cat.'

"If the boy cried, no one saw. He left with the captain for London. He knew there wasn't going to be another cat."

# 23

# The Registered Letter

NOBODY WAS HOME when Fran the postman came with the registered letter. It was addressed to Bernie and Marion, "Guardians of Benjamin—, a minor." Someone had to sign for it. Fran left a slip.

Since Ben and Abby's father was alive and hadn't given his consent, Bernie and Marion couldn't adopt their grandchildren, they could only take care of them. Every few months, a Social Services caseworker came with a checklist and a large file for a home inspection. She had a remote, superior manner that kept Bernie and Marion on edge. Marion was afraid the letter had something to do with their fitness as foster parents.

Marion was a pleasant-looking woman with smile lines. She was not smiling when she showed up at the post office to claim the letter. She was scared. She'd never gotten a registered letter before. From what she'd heard, good news didn't come in registered letters.

She went in, said hello to the clerk, and asked for her letter. Her hand was shaking when she signed for it.

She went out to her car and cut open the envelope carefully, as if it were something important to save.

The letter said that Ben wasn't reading up to grade level and there were problems with his temper. Sometimes when asked to read, he'd throw the book down. He was classified as an "At Risk" student—at risk of failing because of his poor reading. He needed to be tested. Depending on what the test showed, he might need to go to a special class.

That night after dinner Bernie called Ben down to the kitchen for a talk. The boy knew something was up; to be called down to the kitchen after dinner meant trouble.

"The school people know about these things," Marion said. "They figure it will be best for your future."

She knew she couldn't do for Ben what she'd done for Abby. His problems were different.

Abby came running when she heard her brother's long wail. She told Bernie and Marion how the sent-aways were teased. She described the reading sessions in the barn, the vocabulary lists, the verses and sayings he'd memorized, how hard Ben was working to catch up.

Ben's despair frightened his grandparents. It wasn't a boy's rage. It wasn't anger. All feelings he'd built up about his mother's death, his father's being off somewhere and not caring, his inability to keep up with his classmates, gave way at once.

Bernie and Marion were afraid that if they didn't go along with the school's recommendations, they would be reported to Social Services as unfit guardians. As frightened as they were by the violence of the boy's reaction, they didn't want to risk losing him and perhaps his sister too.

Marion didn't hear the boy crying. On instinct she went to him. He was sobbing into his pillow. She put her hands on his head and patted him.

"It will be all right, honey. Things will work out."

He turned over and looked at her.

She smoothed his face until he fell asleep.

# 24

# Ben's School Principal Visits the Texaco

EVERY YEAR the school principal, Dr. Donald Parker, brought his car to the Texaco for its annual inspection because Bernie was fair about it. He didn't look for things to run up a bill. Two days after the letter arrived, Dr. Parker showed up at the station. Bernie had always associated Don with his Ford, but that day when he arrived Bernie saw Don with new eyes: he took him out of his Ford and put him in the school.

Don liked to watch while Bernie checked his car. He didn't get to look at it much himself, so he'd stand under the lift and study what Bernie was tapping and adjusting and peer under the hood when it was up. It was an old car.

As they stood together, Bernie told him about the letter.

"Ben's slow at reading but he's trying to catch up." *Tap tap clunk.* "Sister's helping him." *Twist tap.* "Reading aloud. Word lists. Poems and stuff." *Tap knock twist.*

"Says no to leaving his class. Upset about it. Says he'll get teased. They already tease him about having grandparents for parents."

"Kids can be mean," Don said. "They're always comparing. If you're different, you're going to hear about it, maybe get a nickname. The class fatty, the stutterer, the one with a birthmark, the child who reverses, the one who lisps—they all get teased."

Just then he had to jump back because something Bernie was pulling at let go.

"Ben's had it rough," Bernie said. "Don't tease him."

"Some kids like the attention they get by being different," Don said. "Some of them glory in it and fight back. The teasing makes them work on whatever it is that draws attention. But some are broken by it."

"Better don't break him," Bernie muttered.

"The state says we have to send the letter if a student isn't reading at his grade level. It doesn't mean Ben has to go into Reading Recovery. If he can get his reading up on his own, okay."

Don followed Bernie around to the other side of the car.

"Yeah?" said Bernie.

"He won't improve at all if he's upset," Don said. "But I think RR might help. Gets him out of the pressure of everybody around. Maybe his upset about his mom and dad is getting in his way. Some kids get so mad about stuff like that, they can't see straight. The RR people know how to handle it."

They talked about what Marion had done with Abby. Don told Bernie what went on in Reading Recovery. He suggested Ben sit in on a session.

"He doesn't want to leave his class," Bernie said.

"You don't give up your class if you go into Reading Recovery. It's half an hour a day for twenty weeks. Then they see where you are. We've had pretty good luck with it."

"What about Marion, does she go too?"

"No, this has to be all Ben's."

"What about the test?"

"Tell him I'll make a trade. If he'll observe a Reading Recovery lesson, we'll postpone deciding on whether he has to take the test."

"What about Social Services?"

Don promised to put something in the file with Social Services.

The Ford needed a new brake line.

# 25

# Reading Recovery

AS THE PRINCIPAL drove off, Bernie walked out back on an errand that wasn't an errand. He lit a cigar and wandered slowly among the broken-down cars. There was a clump of cottonwood trees at the edge of the lot. A flicker started a long, clattering call. It sounded like a machine in need of oil.

He was out there for a while. Then he snuffed the cigar, put the stub in his pocket, and went in through the back to where Marion was sorting a stack of grease-marked work orders. He pulled the door. It didn't really shut. The room hadn't been painted in a while. On a high shelf there was a dusty row of model tank trucks and baseball caps marked TEXACO. He sat on the table beside the computer. Marion had the only chair. She'd seen Don come in. She figured they'd talked about the letter.

"Don says he should try Reading Recovery. On his own. Make a trade. If Ben goes to a session, they'll postpone the test."

Over dinner that night Bernie told the family about seeing the principal. Ben's face worked. He didn't say anything. He could hear what they'd whisper if he walked out to go to Reading Recovery. Marion slid her chair over and put her arm around him. Only the two of them knew how hard she squeezed. In important family meetings like this Bernie did the talking. Marion spoke in her own way.

"Dr. Parker said to make sure you've got good light and you sleep enough," Bernie continued. "'Exercise, and no Cokes,' he said."

Down in the barn Whittington was crouched, coughing and heaving. The cat convulsed from end to end for several minutes. The Lady thought he was dying. She went over and stood close to him. Suddenly what was down came up and Whittington shook himself.

"Hairball," he said.

# 26

## Dick Sees a Beautiful Girl in Black

THE FIRST SPRING RAINS washed out the farm road and made a bog of the paddock. The weather blustered. The selectmen posted a flood watch on the river. The pond rose so high it looked like it was going to swamp the road. In the barn the horses were standing in water. Bernie put down extra hay. Water squished up through it. The vet had warned him about hoofrot. He let the horses stand outside while he trucked in sawdust. It didn't do any good; it worked like a sponge. He trucked in gravel. All one Sunday he and the kids wheelbarrowed gravel into the barn to give the horses dry footing. That afternoon they noticed that hair had fallen out in patches on Aramis's back where the skin was pimpled and festering. Bernie called the vet. She said the horse had rain rot and recommended a salve at Agway, an evil-smelling tar that smelled so bad the horse wouldn't try to lick it off. Never mind hoofrot, she said; Aramis should stay tied inside until the rain stopped.

The next morning a stray seagull settled his immaculate gray and white on the pond. Then the water began to retreat and there were tips of new green everywhere.

Ben thought about Dick Whittington. He'd been stuck too. He'd been forced to take a big step because there was no staying where he was. Maybe it was the same for him.

Abby kept the afternoon classes going in the barn. The boy fidgeted. He winced when his sister corrected him. She noticed, though, that every time Ben drew the letter or number he was looking at he read it right. It was as if before he could see it for sure, his hand had to shape it.

The tricks Ben was learning in the barn helped, and the vocabulary. One afternoon Whittington sang a song his master had sung to him. Ben liked it; he thought he could learn it. Abby wrote out the words and taped it below "PSALM":

*The moon on the one hand, the dawn on the other:*
*The moon is my sister, the dawn is my brother.*
*The moon on my left, the dawn on my right*
*My brother, good morning: my sister, good night.*

In two tries he had it. Ben learned the sixteen different words in that song that afternoon. Abby would point to a word with a stick and he'd read it. It didn't matter in what order she pointed, he got them right every time; it

just took him a while to do the sounding out. The Lady noticed the cat shiver. A big thing had happened, or a big thing that had been building was coming into view. Whatever reading was, the boy was doing it. The kids' faces were bright. Abby's eyes were gleaming.

"Okay," said the Lady, feeling surer about the boy than she had for months. "Continue your story, Whittington."

With less effort than it ever took before, the cat leapt back to his storytelling place on the stall rail.

"Dick left his cat in the palace at Tripoli. For days he was too listless to take delight or terror in the fair blue days or the lightning storms with slashing rain. He lay in his bunk. The captain feared he was ill.

"Then one night he was called up to deck to see the rolls of phosphorescence marking the ship's wake. He began sleeping out again. A few nights later, a strange vapor settled around the vessel making her rigging glow with white fire—Saint Elmo's fire it's called. On afternoons when the sea was smooth and chores were done the sailors sang and danced on deck. When they waved for Dick to join in, he did.

"When he got back to London, he was slow letting out his news, not because he was proud but because it pained him. First he showed Fitzwarren the stock he'd bought in Lisbon, then what he'd traded the cat for— bales of cotton, excellent silks, sugar (which was used as a medicine then), gums, drugs, spices. The merchant was pleased; it was all of better quality than any he'd seen before. It would sell at a premium.

"Fitzwarren asked the captain for the waybills. He got the one from Lisbon. There was no bill for the goods from Tripoli. The captain explained that Dick had traded his cat for them.

"'He got that cargo for a cat?'

"'That's not the half of it, but you'd best ask Mr. Whittington.'

"Back home among friends Dick perked up. He sat long with Fitzwarren and the cook telling of his adventures in Barbary, the filthy throne room with the birds, the fortune his cat had won, the strange fire in the rigging. If he told them he missed his cat, they didn't hear it, and if they had they would not have understood. They smiled and laughed. For the cook he had a jewel. He made the old merchant beam when he presented him with the canvas bag of dried *Amapacherie* and the sack of seeds.

"Fitzwarren insisted on paying Dick for the cargo he'd got for his cat and for the dried herb. Only the seeds would he take as a gift.

"The seeds grew, but it turned out that *Amapacherie*—taken as a tea, or eaten, or applied to the body dry or wet, hot or cold—had no effect upon the stone. It may be that in the king's country they took it with something else to make it work. Nobody knew. It was a big disappointment to Fitzwarren because he suffered from kidney stones. He'd experimented on himself.

"Someone told Fitzwarren that what was missing was the ritual that went with taking the medicine. It was a common thing with many of the country people in England then to use spells and incantations to make their medicines work. Other people, using the same herbs and compounds without the rituals, got little benefit or none at all. Fitzwarren's friend thought perhaps it was the same with the *Amapacherie*.

"Dick went to visit the old man who'd sold him the cat. He thought he owed him a share of the fortune. He'd learned that his name was Sir Louis Green.

"There was no easing breeze that afternoon. He arrived at Sir Louis's door red-faced and perspiry. The leather sack he carried was streaked with sweat.

"The old man was again a long time answering. When he did appear, even though it was high summer he was still wearing the long green coat with the brown fur collar turned up. It struck Dick that the green of his coat was like the green stripe across the *Unicorn*'s sail.

"He looked more ancient and wrinkled than before, his face smaller and more sunk down in the fur. His cheeks were pink, though, and he smiled a small, thin smile of pleasure.

"'I've been expecting you,' he said.

"He beckoned Dick inside. His home was dark and cool, the windows shuttered. The furnishings were of the century before and the century before that—dark, gleaming furniture, small objects of glass, rows of silver plate, tapestries hung on walls of carved rubbed oak that smelled of lavender oil.

"Dick was thirsty. Sir Louis led him into a small room lined with manuscripts, maps, and rolled-up charts. On a low table there was a dish of pickled walnuts and two silver tumblers beside a sweating pitcher filled with a sweet, cool drink. A slim girl in black slipped out of the room as Dick came in. He caught his breath when he saw her. 'My granddaughter,' Sir Louis said. They were not introduced.

"Dick told the old man what had happened. He described the fortune he'd gained by the cat and offered to share it. He mentioned that he intended another share for Will Price, the coachman who'd brought him down to London.

"Sir Louis nodded. He seemed to know everything already.

"He wouldn't accept a share of what the cat had won.

"'That's like you, lad,' he said in his piping old man's voice, which was strange since he had no way of knowing what Dick was like.

"'As for Mr. Price,' he continued, 'he is in my employ. I'll give him what you wish.'

"Dick's mouth fell open at the news that the gentleman before him and Will were connected. But before he could say anything the old man made what was for him a long speech.

"'You'll have time enough to give to them as needs. Give them books to learn from, comfort for the sick and old, and bring them water. Clean water, lad.'

"He spoke in a way that did not invite questions or answers, so Dick just nodded.

"Some instinct prompted Dick to trust him. He didn't know what Sir Louis did, or what he had done, but he asked him to take his jewels and gold and invest his fortune.

"The ancient nodded yes. Dick pushed the damp leather pouch across the table. Nothing was counted; there were no papers to sign. Dick gave him what he had, Sir Louis nodded again, that was that."

# 27

# Two Newcomers Join the Barn

WHITTINGTON AND THE LADY looked up when they heard the ducks returning. A pair of mallards settled on the pond before all the ice was out. There were flurries of goldfinches and flurries of snow. The maple knobs turned rust red.

Al, the man who helped Bernie at the Texaco, went to the livestock auction. He didn't need any livestock, he didn't even have a place, but he was curious about goats. When he was a boy, his aunt had kept a pair of white Nubians and a blue-flowered goat cart he got to drive sometimes if he'd drink a cup of goat milk warm from the teats. He'd gag it down and those goats would trot him all over. The more he laughed, the faster they went. The route was theirs. The reins didn't mean anything.

Al went to the library to find out what it would take to keep a goat. He learned they pretty much keep themselves. One book described the goat as a natural emblem of anarchy because it enables a man to live alone. Another said two milk goats can supply most of the food a human being needs, even in the desert.

The auction was held in a barn with wooden pens. There were signs: NO LOOSE FOWL. A flashy rooster was out, though, strutting and crowing. As Al left the parking lot he could hear a chorus of moos, bleats, baas, and squeals. The penned cattle stood patiently; the pigs churned about, sniffing worriedly and nuzzling one another for comfort, grunting and squealing. There was the smell of ordure and stale hay.

The auctioneer chanted high and fast, nothing Al could make out at first. Once the auctioneer got some bidding going he slowed down. A herd of milk goats said to be good for cheese went first, then a long parade of goats. None said "Take me!" to Al. It was five o'clock when they shoved the last one into the ring, a stocky little Alpine. "Do I hear five, five, five, five?" the auctioneer bawled. He didn't hear anything. "Gimme four, four, four, four." Al began to feel bad for that goat; it was like the child left standing alone after the teams are chosen. His hand went up. Someone hauled in the squalling rooster with his feet tied together. He was a dollar. Al said he'd buy him too. His bill came to $5.30 with tax. It was trading money for life.

The auction people offered to tie up the goat's feet so Al could carry it like a suitcase. He said no; he'd manage. He sat it on the front seat and untied the rooster. "You guys sit still," he said. They did. He drove them to the barn.

He tethered the goat to a stanchion so it wouldn't

make the horses nervous. He let the rooster go. When Bernie and the kids arrived the next morning, they found a tied-up goat and a strange chicken. The new rooster was talking things over with Blackie and Coraggio in the rabbit hutch. The goat was stocky and shy, with a steady, unblinking gaze. Its coat was silvery tan with black splashes. It had curving horns, a black beard, mincing feet. The rooster yelled hello and climbed out of the hutch to greet his people like an emperor, stiff and tall with feathered legs and a towering comb of dark coral. He swelled up and let go like a calliope with a five-beat song that was all his own.

"You never know who's going to show up around here," Bernie said to the kids. Since the goat had a beard and horns and something down below, they figured it was a male. It butted like the goat in "The Three Billy Goats Gruff," so they named it William. Ben was for naming the rooster Bronze for his color, but Abby's hearing was fuzzy that morning; she heard him say "Brahms." Given the rooster's talent for music, that became his name. His morning duets with Coraggio got all the neighbors up an hour before sunrise.

Folks in the barn learned to watch and sashay when Willy was around to avoid getting butted. Except for strangers who didn't belong, he didn't hit hard. The problem was the surprise of getting run into. It tickled him to put people off balance.

## 28

## Dick's Cat Returns

THE GOAT STARED unblinking through the reading session. The Lady had more or less told him the story of Dick Whittington up to where the cat was. Willy didn't care about reading, but an adventure story he'd stand around for. If you don't read, you don't get many adventure stories.

The cat jumped back up to his storytelling place. "Where we left off Dick had just returned to London alone but with the excellent goods he'd bought for Fitzwarren, and his fortune.

"Five years went by. Dick took over a greater share of the day-to-day countinghouse business, scouring the docks, seeing to shipments abroad, packing and unpacking, arranging for credit, settling bills. Fitzwarren spent more time in his garden.

"Dick was sixteen. He was tall and strong with a curious scar across his right cheek. He made a fine figure on the docks, jumping into the lighters and wherries and swinging aboard newly arrived vessels. He had purse money of his own. Although he was enrolled with the

Mercers Company as Fitzwarren's apprentice, he was more partner than apprentice. He was becoming a gentleman of name and fortune.

"One day a messenger from Sir Louis appeared at Fitzwarren's shop. He carried a letter summoning Dick to the old man's house at the change of bells that evening.

"Dick went. There were candles on the long waxed table, glasses, a decanter of sherry, and a hard cake that was unlike any Dick had ever tasted. Again he glimpsed the girl he remembered seeing there before, taller now, more woman than girl. He wanted to meet her. Sir Louis gave no opportunity. She did not reappear.

"'It is time you bought a share in Fitzwarren's business,' the old man was saying in his high voice. 'Here is a note with my name and seal. You may draw against me for what money you need. Buy a quarter or three-quarters, but nothing less and nothing more. By no means ever go halves with any man or you will lose both your friend and your money.'

"Dick bought a quarter share in Fitzwarren's business. Fitzwarren wouldn't allow him the larger share he wanted because, he said, he was an old man and when he died the firm would be Dick's anyway. The sum he accepted, he explained, would make his last years easy and provide for the cook, whose knees were bad and getting worse.

"Their trading house came to be known as Fitzwarren and Whittington. Their sign was a dark-striped cat carrying a limp rat.

"Fitzwarren's motto was 'Give value,' and he did. If a customer ordered a pound, he got seventeen ounces; if she ordered a yard, she got three and one-third feet. Any mistake he took to his own account. Dick kept to those rules. Although their prices were not the lowest, the business throve.

"It was now five years since Dick had sold his cat to the king in Tripoli. She would be seven if she was still alive. He thought about her living in the strange, dark palace with the birds. Sometimes he dreamed she was in his room. More than once he awakened, sure she had just jumped on his bed.

"Then one hot afternoon on the wharf Dick spied the captain of the *Unicorn*. Hobbling behind him was the cat. One of her rear legs was bent and shriveled.

"Dick picked her up as if they hadn't been apart for a minute. His eyes moistened. At first he couldn't make his voice work. She began to purr.

"'What happened?' he finally spluttered.

"The cat straightened herself in his arms.

"'The Great Rat took me on.'

"'He attacked you?'

"'I attacked him. I'd tracked him for a long time.

He was bigger than me. We met in his escape tunnel. It was dark and tight. He bit for my spine, the way rats do. I swerved. He got my leg instead and severed the tendon. I turned and tore open his neck. He bled to death. I lost some teeth.'

"Dick had noticed that the cat's mouth was wrinkled, as if she were all the time smiling a puckered smile.

"'I was dragging myself out of his tunnel when his sons got me. They skinned me; my coat was hanging in strips. I kept to my fight discipline, go for the back of the neck, scratch for the eyes. I didn't have bite enough to finish them off. My claws worked, though, so now in Tripoli, instead of three blind mice they have three blind rats. When it was over I was almost dead.

"'A piece of luck saved me. I knew the Great Rat's escape tunnel must have a detour down into one of the palace wells. I found it. It was stinking water, full of salts. The mud around it was even fouler than the water. I tried to drink. I gagged. In my agony I rolled in the mud. It burned all the places where they'd ripped me. Then the hurt went numb. I got caked in mud. I lay there for days. When I was strong enough, I crawled up to the throne room.

"'Himself didn't recognize me. When he did, he called for his doctors and a basin and cloth. He bathed me with his own hands in the cool, sweet water they save for their drinking. I lapped up what was dripping from the cloth. He ordered his own goblet for me to drink from, a thing carved out of rose agate with a handle of gold. It was for his lips only.

"'His doctors couldn't do much,' the cat continued. 'Himself agreed that since I was now useless as a ratter, I might as well go home. I left the palace in care of my children and grandchildren. Himself has plenty of my line to carry on.

"'Anyway, I hear you're for Persia.'

"'Oh?' said Dick.

"'I heard it from the green coat,' said the cat.

"'Sir Louis? You've seen him?'

"'He met us at Land's End. The *Unicorn* is his vessel.'

"'I see,' said Dick. A chill went over him.

He asked the cat, 'If I'm going to Persia, will you go too?'

"She nodded and purred and stretched out a front paw with her toes spread, the way cats do when they're pleased."

# 29

# A Hawk Attacks the Lady

IT WAS A CRISP, clear April afternoon. Suddenly there was a shadow and the Lady screamed. A moment later the crows swarmed, yelling murder.

The Lady had been bathing in her place in the road. No one was around. The red-tailed hawk hadn't been seen all spring, so no one was watching for him, not even Gregory, the local watch crow who had chased the Lady and the cat from the crows' corn party the fall before. Bernie's barn, the pond, and the paddock were his territory. This afternoon he was dozing. The hawk saw his opportunity and dove.

The Lady saw the hawk's shadow an instant before he struck. She made a tremendous leap. He missed her neck. His talons pulled out a clutch of tail feathers. As he rose for another strike, she rushed into the barn. Gregory picked up right away what had happened and started screaming. Crows have an ancient enmity for hawks.

The hawk shifted course when the crow took after him. Crows are fearless. A hawk could kill one crow, but suddenly all the crows in the neighborhood were in pursuit. A gang of crows is like a gang of angry women in a street market after a pickpocket—five of them could do in anyone. The crows put the hawk on the run. With his larger wingspan the hawk climbed faster than the crows could, wheeling higher and higher until he disappeared.

Whittington had been off visiting the tabby in heat down the road. The Lady was cowering in the barn when he returned. The horses told him about the hawk, the crows, the Lady's escape.

Even though it was their favorite thing, the horses had saved some of the molasses grain for her and offered to watch for the hawk if the Lady would come out.

Whittington found her shivering in her nest. She wasn't cold.

"It's okay now," the cat said. "We'll stand guard."

"I saw his shadow," she said. "He almost got me. I felt the wind of his swoop. It was like when he took my brother when we were ducklings. . . ."

She wanted to come out. She was hungry and lonely. The cat would guard her. She heaved into the paddock, more awkward than usual. Her balance was off. The best part of her bustle lay scattered around her bathing place. It would be months growing back.

The horses and the goats stood by her while the cat

watched the sky. The rats crept out to watch the Lady. They were interested in what she'd leave behind.

She ate what the horses had saved for her. Then she went to their bucket and drank in the odd way ducks drink, drawing in a mouthful, then tilting her head up and back to let the water run down her gullet.

Everyone waited for her to say something.

"Oh, my friends . . . ," she began.

Spooker, Aramis, the cat, the goat, the roosters, the bantams, the rats, everyone but Blackie, settled back and waited. She stalled. The Lady was like the boy on commencement day who was supposed to give the class address but couldn't get his wind up. He could only whisper, "Honored guests . . . Honored guests . . ."

That was the awkwardness in the paddock. After her third "Oh, my friends," the Old One yelled, "You including us?"

Startled out of her stage fright, the Lady bellowed, "Yes!" and said her thank-you:

"Oh, my friends, I always wanted a family. You are my family. I rule with your loves. Just as I protect you, so you protect me. I am grateful."

There was a round of cheers. Gregory the watch crow, who thought he'd had a hand in the saving, was disappointed at not being mentioned.

# 30

## Ben Goes to Reading Recovery and Meets Miss O'Brian

BEN'S APPOINTMENT to observe Reading Recovery was a week before Easter. Folks in town had hung out plastic eggs. He was to meet with a reading coach named Miss O'Brian.

Principal Parker took him to the RR room, where a large-eyed boy with dark lashes was slugging it out with "might," writing the letters in boxes Miss O'Brian had drawn on a cardboard strip. Some of the boxes had dotted lines, some solid.

"Mmmmmm-iiiiiii-t," said the boy, sounding it out.

"What do you know about l-i-g-h-t and n-i-g-h-t?" Miss O'Brian was asking. "What do you know about the silent letters in those words?" With her help the boy wrote the silent letters in the boxes with dotted lines. The sounded-out letters got solid-line boxes.

"Okay," said Miss O'Brian. "Now let's sort out these *b*'s and *d*'s." Letters were jumbled on a magnetic board. "Good," she murmured as Keith fumbled to get the *b*'s in their place and the *d*'s in theirs. "Now *w*'s and *m*'s. . . . Okay, now the *a*'s and *e*'s and *p*'s and *q*'s." As Keith struggled, she guided his hand so lightly he wasn't aware of it.

"Now the sand tray." She made it a game. "Draw me a *b*. Good! Quick now, *b, m, w,* five, three, two, *b, p, q, wm, mw, ddbpq.*" The boy's face got red as he struggled and wiped out, her hand guiding his. His letters were crude but you could make them out.

Miss O'Brian asked the boy to write a story. They sounded it out letter by letter as he wrote: "I might make an egg for Mrs. Wright and Sheryl and Sandy." This took a while, with erasing and correcting. She copied his story on another strip of thin cardboard, cut the words apart and jumbled them. Keith had to piece them back together to make his story. She jumbled it again. He sorted again and read his sentence aloud, squinting at the hard words. "Nice job!" Miss O'Brian exclaimed as he got up to leave. He smiled and wiped his face.

Ben stared openmouthed. Somebody else had his problem. Somebody knew how to fix it.

"I'm Miss O'Brian," said the teacher, turning to Ben and putting out her hand. "The kids call me Coach O." Her hand was small and cool. She had a soft voice.

"Let's spend a minute reading together before you go back to your room. How about reading me this?"

Ben did his best. His reading was ragged. She helped him along, smiling, nodding, making notes. "Okay," she said. "You saw us writing in the sand tray. As I say them, draw me these letters."

"Good," she said after a few minutes. "I think I know what's going on. I can help you." She looked at Ben as if she expected him to say something. He said, "Thank you," and left. He knew which boy would make a face when he got back to his room.

# 31

## The Cat's Operation

IT WAS A CLEAR spring afternoon. The school bus let Ben and Abby out at the farm road. It was dim inside the barn, brilliant out, but Abby decided they should keep to their routine and work in the old place. Once they'd dropped their books and run up the street to the corner and back to sharpen up, they ate the snack Bernie had left. Today it was Gran's oatmeal cookies and chocolate milk.

Abby said they should run every afternoon because they didn't have time for sports after school. She had been pretty good at field hockey. Ben liked baseball. During the winter none of their classmates asked where they went every afternoon. Now there were questions. "To work in the barn," they'd say. Friends wanted to come over. They couldn't.

They worked on Ben's reading for half an hour. Abby watched the time. She didn't need to. After half an hour Ben was in a sweat. Then it was Whittington's turn. Sometimes they had to wake him, but he never had to be reminded where he'd left off. He was like a troubadour of old who could continue his story night after night with never a hitch.

"Where we left off," he said, "the cat had just returned. She'd been in a fight with the Great Rat in the palace and lost the use of her right rear leg. Dick had an idea how it might be fixed.

"He asked around for a surgeon who could tie up his cat's tendon. The muscle was withered and might not stretch back, but if the tendon could be restrung, maybe the cat wouldn't have to drag her paw.

"He found a barber who'd done a repair like that for a sailor who'd snapped the cord that runs from your heel to your calf. The sailor's foot flapped. He couldn't walk. The surgeon pulled the two ends together and tied them with silk thread. The sailor couldn't put weight on his foot for a long time; then he had months of exercises to stretch it and put on more load until he could walk again in a rough way.

"'Are you willing to try the operation?' Dick asked the cat. 'It will hurt. I'll have to tie you down and bind your paws because when you feel the knife you'll fight.'

"The cat nodded. 'I'm willing. Anything is better than this.'

"There was nothing to give her for pain. The sailor who'd been operated on had got dead drunk beforehand.

The cat couldn't. Even a little alcohol would kill her.

"They shaved the leg and tied her down. With Dick holding his cat's head and the cat yelling so loud people out in the street looked around, the surgeon cut open the old wound. Hours before, he'd come upon a stray who'd just been crushed by a brewer's cart and taken out its right rear tendon. With the best silk thread he stitched a piece of that tendon to the ends of his patient's severed one. Then he did what he could to line up what remained of the torn muscles.

"Dick treated the cat like the sailor. For the first month her leg was tied to a splint and she hobbled like a tent with one pole too high. For months after that her leg was stiff and useless. Every day the cook applied hot compresses to the leg as Dick pulled and stretched it. Gradually she was able to move it a little, then a little more. It was never right again and the hair never grew back the same color, so that leg looked and worked like somebody else's leg tacked on, which in part it was.

"One curious thing. While his cat was tied down for the operation, Dick noticed that her rear paws were dark purple, almost black. The sacred cats of Egypt had dark purple paws. They were of a rare breed, gods possessed of special powers as protectors of women and guardians of joy. If a house or temple caught fire, the most important thing was saving the cat. When one of those cats died, it was wrapped like a mummy and buried with jewels and food for the afterlife. Carvings were made of them. You can see Egyptian cat figures in museums."

Then Whittington stretched out one of his own rear paws so everyone could see. It was dark purple.

# 32

## Dick Meets Will Price Again

"ONE DAY," THE CAT CONTINUED, "a brisk gentleman appeared in the doorway of Fitzwarren and Whittington's countinghouse. Dick looked up. He had an odd feeling he knew the man by his shape and the way he moved. He couldn't be sure, the face was in shadow.

"His clerk announced a messenger from Sir Louis. It was his old friend Will, the coachman who had brought him to London. It would have been hard to say who was more delighted at the reunion. Arm in arm and with each man talking as fast as he could they made their way to the alehouse.

"Among the hundred amazing things that came out in their excited back-and-forth was that Will had worked for Sir Louis since he was ten. As for the agent who'd been so avid for whipping the country boy at the back of his carriage years ago, he'd died in a fit one morning when his horse stumbled.

"'But I've got to be on to the docks!' said Will. 'Sir Louis has a ship in on the tide. There'll be time enough for us to talk—all the way to Persia, from what I'm hearing. You and the cat are to be at Sir Louis's tomorrow evening at the change of bells.'

"Will was about to leave when he remembered the package at his feet.

"'Sir Louis sent you this book. You're to have it read before you see him tomorrow. He says it will ready your mind for his proposition. He begs you be careful with it because it's his favorite book. He's always reading in it like Scripture and copying out bits. If I could read I'd be into it before the Bible the way he goes on about it.'

"It was a manuscript, a translation of Marco Polo's account of his travels from Venice to Persia and the court of Kublai Khan in China, and on to India and all the places in between.

"A hundred years before Dick Whittington was born Marco Polo had set out from Venice with his father and uncle, merchants like Fitzwarren and Sir Louis, who were searching for new goods and new markets. Marco was seventeen. Travel through the East and on to China was difficult. Few made the trip in Marco's time, few made it in Whittington's.

"Dick read all night and most of the next day. He saw Marco Polo before him, excited and exhausted, one moment telling how hard the journey was, the next how promising. Through Marco's eyes Dick saw strange people:

beautiful women dancing to eerie musics, monks in orange silks, dwarfs, beggars, jugglers, beaters of copper, children weaving rugs, acrobats, jewel traders. He imagined the smell and hubbub of smoky, spice-smelling bazaars with red and yellow tents, magicians in tall hats, seers, snake charmers in costume, camels. He tasted oranges and yellow melons. He smelled the stink of camels' breath. He went through desolate country where squinting warriors on shaggy ponies watched and spat, their speech unintelligible as Marco made the signs for thirst and weariness.

"As Dick shook himself free of its magic, he saw that underneath everything the *Book of Travels* was a businessman's account of customs, sights, and opportunities. Marco described commodities that might find a good market in Europe—silk, drugs, jewels. As for things to exchange, everyone around the world loved gold, coral, fine woolens, oil of rose, ivory, salt."

"Why salt?" Ben wanted to know. "Salt is cheap," he said, pointing to the animals' licking block.

"The salt we get today is," the cat replied. "It comes from mines. In those days it was expensive because they got most of it by evaporating seawater in ponds and skimming off the crystals. The process took a long time. They didn't have refrigeration. They used salt to preserve every kind of meat and fish. They used it in cheese making and leather curing, and to flavor foods. No animal can live without salt. A small gift of it was a handsome present in those days."

"Hmm," said Ben, to whom the notion that there was a time when sugar and salt were hard to come by was as strange as anything.

"Sir Louis knew his man," the cat continued. "The goods Dick read about he imagined trading for as he heard the music in the bazaar and watched the women dancing. He pictured himself riding through mountain passes on squat ponies with the dark, mustached men in costume Marco wrote about. He saw the orange-clad monks and heard their strange, outlandish bells.

"He wondered at the accounts of hashish and opium, and at how in India they practiced 'magical and diabolical arts, by means of which they are enabled to produce darkness. . . .' He read about elephant tusks, almonds, and pistachio nuts. About Persia he read, 'The people are of the Mahometan religion. They are in general a handsome race, especially the women, who, in my opinion, are the most beautiful in the world.'

"He thought of his grandmother and her telling him the Christmas story when he read this: 'In Persia, Marco came to a city called Saba from whence were the three Magi who came to adore Christ in Bethlehem; and the three are buried in that city in a fair sepulchre, and they are all three entire with their beards and hair.'"

# 33

## Willy the Goat's Surprise

SPRING CAME ON FAST. One week flurries, then the grass was tufting up like quilting and there were small yellow flowers. Around the barn chickens were clucking and hurrying about on business. The uproar for a new egg erupted twice, sometimes three times a day. Tractors were out, there were trucks on the highway carrying seed potatoes to the new-turned fields. The horses were rubbing heavily against anything to shed their winter hair. Swallows soared in and out, chattering and calling, gathering horsehair and straw for nests. The nervous phoebe built above the barn door again and scolded every time Bernie or the kids passed underneath.

The goat was edgy. He was growing rounder and rounder. Bernie scolded Al for feeding him so much. "That goat's gonna burst the way you're spoiling him," he growled. Then one day the goat did burst and there was a baby goat, white and wobbly. Bernie rushed back to the station and yelled, "Al, you're an uncle!" Willy became Wilhelmina. Abby named the baby Theo after a boy she liked at school.

As goats go, Wilhelmina was a loving mother. Theo sought her out for what he needed, and got it. He would have done fine without any outside help, but in the eyes of Havey and the Lady, Wilhelmina was barely up to the job. Havey remembered her pups and the Lady thought about children too. The presence of a not-quite-helpless youngster touched their maternal instincts. They took over Theo like two old aunts who had feuded in the past but at last agreed on one big thing. Whittington had ended Havey's attacks on the Lady. Theo made them allies.

Havey sniffed and licked the newcomer from end to end on their first meeting and scrubbed him every day thereafter. Somehow the more helpless the animal, the gentler Havey became. Whatever she'd had to get even about she'd forgotten.

As for the Lady, she had a new student to instruct in the matter of tender greens, things not to get into in the back of the barn, and the history of everyone. Theo was a good student but he jumped. The Lady would be going on when suddenly he'd spring straight up and spin around. He meant no rudeness; that's what young goats do.

The effect of this unique upbringing was to make Theo more careful about his appearance than most goats and picky about his food. He also got quite a high opinion of himself because Al told him everything he had learned about goats in the library.

For all the Lady's instructing, Theo never learned to drink tidily like a duck. Havey's efforts to teach him to run like a dog didn't take either. Right after they'd start a chase together the kid would shoot up, twiddle his legs, then dash off somewhere else.

Coraggio's singing lessons were more successful. Theo would join the rooster at dawn with a long, deep *baa*. Their music made Bernie smile as he drove in.

# 34

# Dick Sees the Girl in Black Again

DICK WHITTINGTON was in Ben's dreams and daydreams. School was in his nightmares. For all Abby's work in the barn, he was still behind his classmates. While he'd been making progress, they had been too. They were getting further and further ahead.

One afternoon the cat noticed that the boy was tired and angry. "What's up?" he asked.

"In reading some guy teased me, said I sounded like an air compressor—*ppppaaapppttt.* I slugged him."

There was a cheer from the rats.

"I got sent home. It's not fair."

"What about the classes with Coach O?" the cat asked.

"Dr. Parker says I'd have to go all summer. Everybody would know."

"In school everybody knows everything about everybody anyway," Abby said.

"They'll say things," Ben growled.

There was a heavy silence. The horses chewed and

made the thoughtful snuffling noises horses make sometimes. The chickens dozed. The goats were indifferent. Goats don't think much about anyone else.

"You're stuck," the Lady said. "Stay where you are and what's going to happen?"

The rats were rooting for the boy to sign up. The Old One fixed Ben with his one bright bead eye and said, "I would if I could. From what I've heard out of Abby's books, there's more world out there in books than in this barn and field and all of Northfield ten times over."

The cat gave Ben a long look. "The boy in my home before didn't have your chance."

Maybe it was then that Ben decided to take his chance. He didn't say anything. He made a fist.

Whittington jumped up to his storytelling place. He waited until Ben relaxed his hand. He knew the boy wouldn't be able to hear until he did.

"Dick's old friend, the coachman who'd brought him down to London years before, had reappeared. He'd been sent by Sir Louis with a book. Dick was to go to Sir Louis's the next evening having read it. He'd been up all night reading Marco Polo's *Travels*. He finished it just before he set out.

"The cat went along. She'd recovered from her operation but she was limping.

"She was too proud to be carried, so the young man walked slowly. He was eighteen now, tall and strong, clean-shaved, with a chiseled face, deep blue eyes, and long, curling blond hair. There was a thin white scar across his right cheek.

"As the cat hobbled along behind him, passersby thought it cruel that the fine gentleman didn't bother to pick up the devoted pet limping at his heels. Dick knew the bite he'd get if he tried. In fact, the cat was walking better and better.

"Will let them in. Sir Louis's house was ablaze with candles. Dick was shown to the old man's study. The cat slipped in on her own. There was a fire in the room. Sir Louis was in his green coat with the fur collar turned up. Maps were spread out on every table. Fitzwarren was there, the captain of the *Unicorn,* some other gentlemen Dick did not recognize, and Sir Louis's granddaughter, the slim young woman in black Dick had seen twice before.

"There were introductions. The strange men were three old sea dogs, ship captains who'd had experience sailing the Dardanelles and the Bosporus. The sailing charts belonged to them.

"Some might not have found the girl beautiful. Dick could hardly breathe for looking at her. She was tall, with long black hair that gleamed in the candlelight.

She had a quick smile. Her eyes were bright and lively like a bird's eyes. Her mouth was large, she had a fine nose. She felt his stare and reddened, the pink showing under the faint olive cast of her skin. She slipped from the room like a shadow. The cat followed her.

"Dick jumped up. 'My cat!' he said. In the dim passage he bumped into the girl.

"'I am . . . You are . . . My cat . . .' His tongue wouldn't work.

"'In the pantry,' she said, laughing. 'She smells the forcemeat.'

"She took his hand. 'This way.' Her silks rustled softly. Dick could smell her hair, her rose scent.

"In the candlelit pantry they found the cat. She was waiting for them on a servant's stool. It was as if she'd led them on. She wasn't eating. The girl picked her up and stroked her.

"'I'm Dick Whittington,' he said.

"'I know,' she replied. 'Grandfather speaks of you. I'm Mary Green.'

"'Yes,' he said. He had a hundred things to say but he couldn't speak.

"For a moment the only sound was the cat's purr.

"'We must go back,' Mary said. Her voice was low. To Dick it was like music.

"'May I see you again?' he asked.

"She looked down and shook her head. 'No.'

"Pale and shaken, Dick rejoined the party.

"What the talking came to was this: Sir Louis wanted Dick to sail with a shipload of English woolens and German salt and establish a factor, or agency for trade, at Constantinople. If he could make it into Persia, he was to establish another station at Tabriz. He would be retracing part of Marco Polo's route.

"Sir Louis had a charter from his friend and debtor, King Edward. Not that a piece of handsomely written-on parchment with ribbons and red wax seals would carry much weight with sea pirates, viziers, pashas, and the sultan who controlled the narrow blue straits that separate Europe and Asia. They would need cajoling with gold. Dick would have gold. The men said that if he could open agencies in those places, it would be a great thing for England.

"Each of them had a share in the venture. If Dick succeeded, it would be a great thing for them too.

"'Your share will be enough to make you rich beyond the dreams of avarice,' said one of the captains. 'And you'll be risking no capital of your own.'

"'Except your life,' said Fitzwarren, almost to himself.

"A day before, an hour before, the young man's

blood would have thrilled to talk of trade and silk routes, gold and glory for England and himself. But now he could hardly pay attention. He was burning. He kept looking for the girl.

"The talk droned on until at last the men progressed to dinner. Mary joined the party. The cat settled in her lap as servants passed cold beef tongue in horseradish sauce, peas in lard, small birds roasted in pastry, a soup of berries, sweet white wine, dishes of shaved ice with red syrup. Dick ate nothing. He couldn't swallow. His eyes were like lions for that girl. He took in her face, the shade of her cheeks, the graceful way she moved with not a motion wasted. He could just make out her body, young and firm, the body of a girl who walked miles and rode her own horse.

"Her eyes were on him too, although he didn't know it. She was discreet in her looking. His cat purred and purred, kneading the girl's thigh, the way cats do to say something. Had Mary been able to understand Dick's cat, it would have told her, 'Love comes in at the eyes.'"

# 35

## Marker Raids the Barn

THE DOG THAT LIVED in the house at the top of the farm road was a coal-and-chocolate Border collie with a blunt brown muzzle and white paws. Marker was bred for herding but he'd had no training. He didn't get much exercise. He was frantic to run and chase. His one delight was going out early with his mistress. Sometimes she walked him toward the barn. He wanted more than anything to herd that crowd.

One morning he slipped his leash and tore down the farm road. He took a turn through the paddock to send the horses running, as he'd watched Havey do so many times. Then he swept into the barn. The Lady scooted deep into the dark back under junk. Brahms flew high with the screeching bantams.

Coraggio was struggling to get up on his hay bale when the dog got him by the neck. Feathers were flying like someone emptying a pillow when Wilhelmina butted Marker broadside so hard the rooster was blown free. Coraggio staggered and collapsed. The dog was struggling up when the cat sprang, clawing his eyes. As Marker's mistress came shrieking to his rescue,

Wilhelmina slammed him again. He was carried whimpering up the hill.

When Bernie showed up, he knew something was wrong. Nobody was out. It was silent in the barn. Everyone was standing around Coraggio. He lay where he'd fallen. The tall man stooped and shook his head. "Nature is mean," he muttered. There was no blood.

Havey nosed the body.

Bernie kicked at the dog. "Leave it alone," he said. But Havey kept nuzzling the limp rooster and licking him. Coraggio stirred, raised his head, flopped back, then struggled to get up. He couldn't.

The tall man's face was a study in wonder as he looked at the wagging dog and lifted the fluttering chicken into Blackie's cage.

It was a week before Coraggio could stand on his own again. His wonderful voice was ruined forever but soon everything else about him was working fine. Thereafter, first thing when Havey arrived at the barn she would give him a lick.

Al said that Coraggio had had the breath knocked out of him. It was a common thing with birds that flew into windowpanes. All they needed was to rest a little and they'd revive.

Bernie knew otherwise. "That chicken was dead. Havey did something."

# 36

# Dick Decides on the Dangerous Voyage

IT WAS A DRIZZLY afternoon when Whittington resumed his story. The animals had come in. It smelled of wet horse, wet chickens, last summer's hay, manure.

"Where we left off, Sir Louis and his friends wanted Dick to make a trip like Marco Polo's. At the dinner where they laid out their plan Dick saw Mary again.

"Sir Louis had guessed Dick's interest in Mary. Over dinner he announced that he had arranged for her to marry a gentleman of an old titled family. Dick felt sick. He tried to catch her eye. He could see that her face and neck were burning. She kept her eyes down.

"Sir Louis went on about how important the voyage was for England. His words blew over Dick like so much wind. The cat pawed at his leg. He lifted her into his lap. She began to purr. He didn't notice. She clawed gently; finally she bit him. She had something to tell him. For the first time he couldn't hear what his cat had to say. There was too much news: news of fortune, news of disappointment. Sir Louis had picked a husband for the lovely girl. More than anything in the world Dick wanted to be alone with her."

"What did the cat want to tell him?" Ben asked.

"Nothing specific, just that she had a good feeling about the future. Dick couldn't hear her. His ears buzzed like someone in fever.

"Weeks went by. He couldn't decide about the venture. His old friend and partner was of two minds about it too. Fitzwarren was past sixty now. He liked to work in his garden and relied on Dick to handle their business. He feared that if Dick made the trip, he might not see him again. Folks regarded the strapping lad as his son. Fitzwarren had come to think of him that way too.

"Still, Fitzwarren was as curious as he was fearful. He had the true English spirit for risk-taking. Among other curiosities, Dick might encounter rhubarb and lilac on his way, two plants that were much wanted. Rhubarb is cooked into sauces, pies, and jams now. In Dick's time the dried root was imported at great price to relieve constipation because the diet then was mainly meat and bread. Vegetables and salads were not popular. One cure for sluggish bowel was a purge of powdered rhubarb root in honey water.

"Dick had managed to obtain seeds of the *Ama-pacherie*. Perhaps he would be as lucky with rhubarb. Fitzwarren wrote to a friend about it. What he heard back was not encouraging: 'The Country where the True Sort Lyes is so remote between China & Tartary that to procure it is almost Impossible, because no Europeans that I can learn trade thither. It is brought by the natives to Russians, who lay nearest & have engrossed that Trade. . . .'

"As for lilac, travelers from Algiers described a tall bush with heart-shaped leaves and bunched clusters of fragrant purplish-blue blossoms that perfumed an entire garden for weeks. According to one tradition, its name is Persian for 'beautiful girl.' Fitzwarren longed to have it. He pressed his thumb against his nose and said Dick should go.

"The more he thought about her, the more deter-mined Dick became to see the girl in black. Will reported that she'd been sent to Sir Louis's country place ten miles outside London. He added that her suitor was a gentleman of rank and Dick should leave well enough alone.

"The morning he was to advise Sir Louis, Fitzwarren, and the captains of his decision about the voyage, Dick set out on a different trip. He started walking up the Thames towpath to Richmond to find Mary.

"The tide was coming in. The river surged like a pulse, noisy and slicking, carrying branches, leaves, and trash. At places it surged across the path. His cat tried to follow. She couldn't keep up.

"Dick was unkempt. His step was not steady. He saw things and heard things in the river noise. Sunday bells began to ring. They filled his head—deep bells, long bells, bells with silver, bells of bronze. In their rhythms there was a message that seemed to come at him from every direction: 'Turn around, Dick Whittington, turn around.' He kept walking like a man drunk. Then the river quieted and all the bells stilled but one, a harsh, dry bell that called up his grandmother's face. It tolled one word: 'Back. Back.'

"He turned around. He was sobbing as he had never done before in his life. Stumbling back down the river path, he met his cat. He stooped to pick her up. He would never forget the beautiful girl, but the strange fever that had possessed him had broken."

# 37

## Ben's Decision

AT THE SPRING parents-and-teachers meeting, Ben's teacher told Marion she didn't think he should pass. His attendance was almost perfect, he made no trouble, he picked up things they discussed in class. If he heard something, he would learn it. The problem was his reading. More and more classwork would be in books. If Ben couldn't read with the others, he wouldn't be able to manage.

"I'm amazed what he can memorize, though," she said. "He's the best in the class at that. When it's time for free discussion, the other kids always ask him to recite. Almost every time he has something new."

When Marion got home, she told Ben about the meeting. He didn't seem surprised or upset. She didn't know what to make of that.

The next afternoon he told Abby and the barn, "Mrs. Wright told Gran they're going to keep me back. They aren't. Coach O has twenty sets of books I have to work through. She says if I'm reading in set twenty by the time school starts next fall, she'll recommend I stay with my class. She thinks I can do it if I start RR in May when school lets out. It's fourteen weeks, my whole vacation. . . ." His voice dropped when he got to the vacation part.

Abby whooped, the cat's tail went up, the horses snorted. There were cheers from all corners.

"You're going to be our missionary," the Old One said. When he put it like that, Ben no longer felt bad about being one of the sent-aways and giving up his vacation. He'd send himself. He'd be the missionary.

The cat had seen it coming, he'd helped it along. He wasn't going to lose this boy.

"You're taking charge of yourself like Dick Whittington," the Lady said. All hearts were full.

# 38

## A Token for Mary

"THE STORY!" "THE STORY!" they shouted. Whittington jumped up to his storytelling place.

"Dick sailed from London in the cog *Unicorn* with Will Price, the cat, a rich cargo, and a crew of twenty. Their sail bore Sir Louis's sign, the green stripe across the top. At the top of the lead halyard they flew the red cross of St. George.

"Dick carried with him the charts Sir Louis had gathered from the captains and the Marco Polo book. Sir Louis had not wanted to give it up. He read in it every day. When Dick said he wouldn't go without it, Sir Louis stared at him for a long moment. Then he nodded slowly and wrote on the inside cover, 'For Richard Whittington, his *vade mecum*,' which means the book he kept beside him for daily use.

"Dick wasn't himself the first weeks out. His face was hollow, he went about like a sleepwalker. But they had clear sailing and this time he wasn't seasick. Gradually the sun and chores on shipboard got him out of himself. After a while he could hear his cat again. She said, 'It will all work out.'

"They made for Palermo in Sicily, where Greeks, Phoenicians, and Romans had traded for three thousand years. Palermo was a hive, one of the major ports of the world, with ships in from Africa and the East every day. Dick hoped to learn about rhubarb and lilac and other new things there, and trade for goods and commodities unknown in England. He'd picked up enough Italian and Arabic to make his needs known. He was used to speaking with sailors and dockhands from all over the world in the universal language of single words, figures, signs, and gestures. Sailors knew things before they got marked on charts and written in books.

As they approached Palermo, the sailors watched for the square gold seamark rising against the mountains over the port and the dark green orange groves. Their ship bore straight toward it, the gold square of Monreale, the ancient church built by an Englishman.

"Shortly after they docked, Will came down with a wasting fever that made him sweat and shake and turned him yellow. It would let up for a few weeks, then surge back. He looked like a skeleton. Marsh fever, it was called then; today we know it as malaria. Dick was sure it would kill him and Will said as much. Dick knew without being told that Will wished to die with his family around. He arranged for the captain to take him home in the *Unicorn*. He gave the captain a blue silk shroud to use if he had to bury Will at sea.

"Dick told Will he was sending him home. The two men embraced.

"'You were my first true friend,' Dick said. He didn't try to hide his tears.

"Will smiled through his. 'You've been a good friend to me, boy, almost kin, like I told old Radish Face you was. Didn't we give *him* a time!'

"While the captain hurried to provision the *Unicorn* for her return voyage, Dick found traders who had lilac and other strange plants to delight Fitzwarren. One was rosemary, popular in Sicily for flavoring roast meats but not yet grown in England. Nobody had live rhubarb. Small quantities of dried root were available but no seeds.

"It was late January, the time of year when the wild white narcissus blooms on the Sicily coast. Its blossoms are the size of snowflakes. Their sweet scent fills a room. Dick spent days gathering bulbs for Fitzwarren. He wrapped the bulbs, lilac roots, and other rare plants tight against weather and salt spray and put them in Will's care.

"He traded the *Unicorn*'s cargo of woolens and salt for its value in spices, wine, olive oil, cotton from Egypt, sandalwood, which was prized for carving and incense, tamarind, peacock feathers, saffron, pieces of carved ivory and jade, and a small sack of pearls.

"The spices in their sealed casks were the most valuable part of the cargo. Salt was one preservative at that time; spices were a welcome alternative. Used alone and in mixtures, they were prized because they held off bacteria, fungi, and parasites and masked the smell of rot. Clove, nutmeg, cinnamon, mace, and ginger brightened all sorts of foods.

"Two days before the ship was to sail, the cat told Dick, 'Send home a token for Mary with this message: If you don't know me, you know nobody.'

"'Send her a token?' Dick exclaimed. 'If you don't know me . . .'? What does that mean? How would it look? What would Sir Louis say? She is probably a married woman now. . . .' He broke off.

"'Go to the shell carvers,' said the cat. 'They are famous here. Tell them as best you can what she looks like, her coloring, the shape of her head, her particular nose, the way her chin curves. Have them carve her face in a fine piece of shell. Don't sign the note. She will know who sent it.'

"'But why?'

"'Go quickly,' the cat said, and then she disappeared.

"Safe in the captain's cabin, tucked among the plant parcels for Fitzwarren, there was a small box tightly sealed in parchment. When Fitzwarren unwrapped it, he read, 'Pray, friend, have this delivered to Mary with no hint from whence it came.' Inside the box was a cameo, an oval of seashell carved in the image of the young woman's face. It was framed in gold with a clasp. It was wrapped in the note the cat had dictated: 'If you don't know me, you know nobody.'"

## 39

## Gent Arrives

EARLY ONE MORNING there was a strange honking over the barn, a sound no one had ever heard before. The Lady half flew out of the barn, uttering yawps that were altogether new.

A brown and tan duck called and circled and finally landed on the pond. He came to shore to meet the Lady, moving his head from left to right, bowing and singing. When she murmured something in response, he turned and invited her to meet him on the water, where they could be private. She sailed out. For hours they clucked and honked at each other, then they billed and twined necks. From that day on they were inseparable.

The Lady introduced him to the barn. His name was Gent. He was polite but shy. Somehow he'd got separated from his flock. There was no asking if he could become part of the family. The Lady said they were made for each other.

Gent was not much for conversation in the barn. He'd come in when Bernie put down the sweetened grain, then he'd be off to swim and waddle along the pond margins eating shoots. He said he came from the south, where winters were mild and all the ducks returned at year-end. That puzzled the Lady, but she let it go.

Within a month of his arriving she laid her first egg. A week later another egg appeared, then a third. The kids found them on their daily hunt for bantam eggs. The duck eggs were twice as large.

Gent and the Lady spent their days sailing the pond, carving long, languid sweeps through the green weed that dotted the surface, pulling up delicious roots, chuckling and grunting to each other. She gave him all her attention. She didn't ignore Whittington, she just didn't have time for him.

Whittington didn't have a best friend anymore. He felt like Dick's cat after her master fell in love with the girl in black. Only at dusk would the Lady come inside. Gent stayed out. He could fly in an emergency; she could not. The cat still slept beside the Lady by the barn door, but her conversation was all about Gent and life on the pond.

Bernie said a few eggs should be left for the bantams to brood. The chickens were eager to settle on their eggs. Despite her maternal instincts where Theo the goat was concerned, the Lady ignored hers.

Abby tried to get a bantam hen to sit on one. It was too large to be comfortable, she couldn't keep her balance. On an inspiration Ben tucked two duck eggs in the rabbit hutch. Blackie was a full-sized hen. She was delighted to have eggs to brood. She hopped and bustled and took them on as her own. When Bernie added the third, she spread her wings to keep the clutch covered.

A flock of bantam chicks came, then two ducklings. The Lady was pleased, but she continued to spend her days on the water. Every morning Ben would lift the ducklings out of the hutch. The bantams led their chicks around, Brahms and Coraggio led the baby ducks. They taught them preening, how to drink, the wonderful things to be found in the dung heap, everything about dust baths. Blackie watched and fretted. While she admired Brahms for the way he exercised his musical authority, she didn't think much of his mothering skills.

One morning as Ben was lifting the ducklings out of the hutch, Blackie gave a tremendous flapping jump, cleared the opening, and plopped down among her charges. Thereafter the three chickens paraded the ducklings together, the large bronze rooster yelling their advance, the black hen hopping along on one side, two oddly marked ducklings peeping. With Coraggio bringing up the rear, they'd make a long, slow turn around the paddock, visit the dung heap, then head to the pond, where the Lady took over. The three chickens worried at the water's edge until the Lady brought the ducklings back. Chickens can't swim.

On the hottest afternoon in August the tabby down the road carried her two kittens to the barn, first one, then the other, squirming and complaining. One looked like Whittington. They were underfoot in the home where she lived. She had overheard that they were to be taken to the pound. She figured the barn would be better than that. So now Whittington had his own little ones to watch and train. He didn't have his best friend to himself anymore, but he was too busy to be lonesome.

As for Ben's reading, from ten to eleven-thirty every weekday he worked with Coach O. He learned more than reading. The third morning, when he stalled, he threw the book across the room. Coach O sent him home. He thought she'd call Gran. She didn't. He wasn't sure when he showed up the next morning that she'd see him. She acted as if nothing had happened. For the rest of the week, though, she kept him until noon to make up the time he'd missed.

A week later, when he got tangled up shaping letters in the sand tray, he dumped it in a fury. Coach O pursed her lips and said, "Go run twice around the playing field as fast as you can."

When he came back in, red-faced and panting, she pointed to the mess of sand. "Clean it up," she said.

Thereafter he had to get to school at nine-thirty to run laps before the reading session. "Exercise will save you when you feel like exploding," she said. "It changes the subject. It's real hard to get mad at yourself after a good sweat."

It worked. Ben didn't blow up again.

# 40

# A Rescue

A FEW NIGHTS LATER, Whittington was out. It was late. Kittens are night creatures too. His two children were rolling on the barn floor, playing in a tangle of old hay bale cords.

Bales were piled above the kittens. A loose cord dangled. One bale wasn't stacked tight against the others. It was balanced to make it easy for Bernie to pull it down in the morning.

The kittens wrapped themselves in the tangle on the floor and fought over the dangling cord. They pulled the bale down. They saw it coming and jumped aside, but it fell on the tangle, snagging one of the kittens. A cord was looped tight around her throat. She lay choking on the barn floor.

The horses gave the alarm. The Lady rushed over and pecked at the cord. She couldn't loosen it.

"Rats!" she yelled. "Help! Rats! Help!"

The Old One came running. He saw how it was and started to gnaw and pull at the strangling cord.

Finally he severed it and freed the kitten.

She lay panting on the barn floor.

The Lady looked her over.

"She'll be okay," she said. "Just lost one of her nine lives. Thanks, rat."

"Tit for tat," said the Old One.

## 41

# Dick's Cat Is Lost at Sea

ABBY AND BEN came to the barn twice a day, first with Bernie for the morning feeding at five, then on their own on bikes in the afternoon for the cat's story. It was hot in the barn but that's where they wanted to be. Gent stayed out on the water. The Lady came in with her ducklings. The bantams and the chicks were there, the roosters, Theo and his mama, the two horses. Whittington's kittens watched as he leapt up to his storytelling place. There was a large crowd looking up.

"At Palermo Dick chartered a caravel to take him east to Constantinople. Although the caravel was newer and sleeker than the *Unicorn,* they barely made it. A squall in the Dardanelles smacked the ship so hard her masts snapped. The sailors who were trying to furl the sails were swept overboard. The deck was a mess of splintered wood, torn sail, and tangled rigging. There was no sign of the cat. No one saw her go overboard. She'd been on deck moments before. She wasn't steady on her feet. She could not have withstood the rush of wind and water that heeled the ship so far over it nearly capsized.

"Dick combed the wreckage looking for her. There was no trace. In his bunk she'd left two mewing kittens, newborns. Their eyes weren't open yet. Had their mother been on board, she would have made it to them no matter how injured she was. That's the way it is with cats. One of those kittens was my forebear.

"He'd lost Mary and Will, and now he'd lost his cat, but he was too busy staying alive to think much about his losses. He went to the side of the ship and untied the blue silk he wore around his neck. He wiped his face and tossed it overboard as a token for the cat.

"There was nothing for it but to take his shifts at pumping and help the exhausted crew jury-rig the ship so they could get to port. He remembered one of his grandmother's maxims, 'Work is the medicine for despair.' He worked day and night, taking breaks only to tend the kittens. They weren't weaned, they couldn't drink from a dish, they didn't know solid food. The goats saved them."

Wilhelmina and Theo pricked up their ears.

"The sailors had on board two fresh she-goats, which means they had just had babies and were giving milk. The custom among sailors in that time was to drink their milk as long as they gave it, then butcher them for meat. The goats had survived the storm in their tied-down cage. The kittens owed their lives to those goats and so do I.

"Dick put some goat milk in a cup, dipped his finger, and pushed it into a tiny mouth. The kittens were starving. Goat milk is rich. It made them strong. As he fed and watched them, Dick told the kittens the story of their mother, everything he knew. As they grew up, what they wanted to know most of all was her name and how she had happened to turn up on Sir Louis's doorstep the afternoon Dick saw her for the first time. He didn't know.

"As his battered ship crept through the narrow blue strait to Constantinople, Dick looked over to Asia. A person could swim across. The land of Marco Polo lay beyond in a blue glow. It reminded Dick of the moment in his first voyage sailing past Gibraltar and seeing the red haze of Africa.

"While his ship was refitting at Constantinople, he saw to the opening of the agency there, as Sir Louis and his backers had wanted. That work done, he put the kittens in his pocket and spent days wandering the city. It was the grandest he'd ever seen, a vast walled fortress filled with gilded domes and temples. The chief one, the Hagia Sophia, seemed to be a city unto itself, a huge space under a weightless golden shell filled with pictures made of colored stones.

"Outside there were voices and laughter, friends yelling to friends, flutes wailing, merchants singing their wares, men playing stringed instruments and beating cymbals, women dancing to the rhythms of skin-covered drums.

"The smells of meat cooking made him hungry. At the food stalls he bought chunks of grilled spiced lamb on a stick and dishes of curried grains. The grains were strange. They were rice. He fed the kittens small bits of lamb he'd chewed to paste.

"In the bazaar at the Golden Gate he bought a carved turquoise bead strung on a thong of black leather. It was a thin cylinder from Tibet. 'A sacred relic,' the woman who sold it said as she tied it around his neck. 'It will bring what you desire above all else,' she whispered.

"He bought large woven sacks of figs, dates, and rice, and casks of oil and spices. He walked the docks hunting for merchandise that would sell for a good profit in London. Everywhere he asked for rare plants, especially rhubarb for Fitzwarren. Some knew the dried root, but no one had seen the growing plant. From traders to China he heard report of a vegetable curd popular there, a sort of cake called *tau-foo* made from a pea. He knew that would quicken Fitzwarren's heart, so he offered a large reward for the pea and the recipe for the meat made of it. No one took it up. Today we know that 'pea' as soy and the food as tofu.

"He gathered lengths of Indian silk and cotton cloth. He found bright patterned rugs tied knot by knot by the desert people and implements of bright beaten copper and bronze. From an Afghan trader he bought a handful of gem-shaped orange carnelians for the jewelers in London, and chunks of lapis lazuli, the deep blue rock painters grind fine to paint sky. The Afghani had small, shiny blocks of gum arabic for sale too, the dried resin of a tree that painters dissolve to use as a medium for the ground lapis.

"Dick inquired about sailing east across the Black Sea and then going overland south to Tabriz in Persia. After his reading Marco Polo, the name Persia sounded in his head like a poem. He didn't have enough money. What with the costs of chartering and refitting the caravel, acquiring the cargo of trade goods, and establishing the agency, he was almost out of gold and credit. He promised himself he'd try again.

"On the way home, as his ship passed Land's End at the southwest tip of England, Dick sent word by land to Fitzwarren. A week later, when his vessel finished her reach up the Channel and finally got a favorable wind on an inflowing tide up the Thames, his old friend was on Limehouse Wharf to welcome him like Joseph returned from Egypt. It was Dick's twenty-second birthday.

"They embraced and talked for hours in a dark tavern over mugs of warm ale, a joint of roast mutton hot from the spit, black bread spread thick with butter. Dick hadn't tasted butter in months. It tasted wonderful.

"Fitzwarren had news of Will's dying at sea. Dick told about the squall in the Dardanelles, the agency at Constantinople, the gold-domed temple there, the cargoes. He didn't mention his cat.

"When he asked about the package he'd sent for Mary, Fitzwarren's face wrinkled.

'A month after you sailed she married the gentleman, as was planned. Not half a year on, not far from here, he was kicked in the gut by a cart horse gone wild. He lingered for a few days, in agony but lucid enough to make his last will and testament, giving the Church all that he had, including her dowry portion.'"

"What does that mean?" Abby asked.

"It means he signed over to the Church everything he owned, including the property Sir Louis gave him to marry her. That gift is called a dowry. It was the custom then for people of Sir Louis's class to buy their daughters or granddaughters a socially advantageous marriage by settling a valuable gift on the husband. Fathers bargained their children for marriage like they were buying and selling properties."

Abby made a face.

"'All of that happened more than a year ago,' Fitzwarren said. 'Sir Louis took care of Mary after her husband died. When your package arrived, she was still in mourning, so I debated passing it on. I had an idea you'd keep after her, but I didn't think it right. I was going to take the matter up with Sir Louis. Then I looked at your note again. You asked me to deliver your package. I did so with my own hand.'

"'Not long after, Sir Louis passed away. They said he was in his ninety-third year. He'd named me one of his pallbearers. I didn't know he esteemed me so as a friend. It's a hard thing to learn you were treasured by someone you admired only after he's cold.' Fitzwarren shook his head and looked away."

# 42

## Mary

"THE NEXT DAY Dick sent a note to Mary asking if he might visit. She wrote back yes. He met her at Sir Louis's country home in Richmond, the place he'd been walking to in hopes of seeing her when the bells had called him back. She was wearing his token. The carved shell was a startling likeness.

"He'd gone up with his two cats. They went everywhere with him. As he sat with Mary in the garden, one cat left Dick's lap and went to Mary's, where it settled as if it had been there forever. There was the fragrance of roses.

"Dick and Mary talked until the sun went down and moths came flickering. Dick took Mary's hand. It fluttered like a moth. Then it settled into his.

"He told her about seeing her the first time, the afternoon he called on Sir Louis after his voyage to Africa. He described the birds in the king's throne room at Tripoli where the cat had won him a fortune, the ancient temple at Palermo that caught the sun at dawn, the scent of wild white narcissus blooming on the rock coast there, the glittering wonders of Constantinople. He untied the black thong with the turquoise bead and put it around her neck.

"She touched his face gently, tracing his scar.

"'How did you get it?' she asked.

"He told her about riding to London on the land agent's carriage with Will Price. He told her about his grandmother.

"'You didn't say goodbye to her?'

"'She knew,' he said softly.

"Mary told him her parents had died of plague before she was old enough to know them and how Sir Louis had raised her and arranged her marriage. She told him about Fitzwarren coming with his package.

"'I knew it was from you before I opened it. It made me joyfuller than I'd ever been in my life.'

"They married and had a mostly happy life together, with one daughter. Dick Whittington prospered and became lord mayor of London, just as the coachman, Will Price, had predicted on the carriage so many years before.

"Dick kept Marco Polo's book beside him always, but he never left England again. He never made it to Tabriz.

"He lived to a great age, surviving his wife and daughter. As an old man his companion was his cat, a descendant of the great ratter. People found it strange that as he and his cat walked together, they seemed to be talking.

"In his last years he spent his fortune on a public library, a hospital, and an almshouse for the poor. His biggest project, though, was the one Sir Louis had dreamed of—laying pipe to carry clean water to spigots in the slums.

"He is not remembered because he died rich. He is remembered because he gave away everything. And everything he had to give away he owed to his cat.

"That's as much as I know," said Whittington. "I got the story from my mother, who got it from her mother—up the chain, mother to daughter, mother to daughter, all the way back to Dick Whittington's cat."

Nobody said anything. As swallows coasted in and out of the barn, the silence in that heat was like sand falling.

# 43

# Ben's Triumph

BEN FINISHED the last Level 19 book the Friday before Labor Day. School was to start the day after. Coach O called Dr. Parker.

"He's got the Level 20s to do, but he's there. Move him up."

Dr. Parker called Bernie at the Texaco.

"Ben did it! He's going on with his class."

"Thanks" was all Bernie could manage.

He went over to Marion's room. She left work so fast she forgot to shut down the computer. Ben liked her angel food cake best of all. He was going to have all the angel food he could eat.

Ben knew before anybody. Coach O had told him. He headed to the barn. "I did it!" he yelled. "I'm not going to stay behind or anything." Abby was laughing and crying, the rats danced, the horses tore around the paddock with tails flying like it was a race day. The cat swelled up bigger than the day he'd given Havey her surprise. Brahms crowed so long and hard he got dizzy and fell over. The bantams ruckused, Theo sang like it was dawn. All was jubilation, dust, and pandemonium.

The Lady called for order. "We all had a hand, a wing, and a paw in this. It isn't just Ben, we've all passed!" There erupted such a whooping cheer that Gregory the watch crow came over to find out what was going on.

# 44

## Life in the Barn Continues

THE LADY AND GENT were happy together until the first sharp winds of autumn brought flights of ducks over, calling loudly as they headed south. When Gent called back, some of the fliers wheeled low and yelled to him to come along. He flew up with his children and joined them. He circled twice, honking to the Lady. She squalled and flapped but she couldn't go. Then it was quiet. Everyone was looking up. The sky was empty.

Suddenly she felt old and exhausted. She dragged herself to her sleeping place by the barn door and quit eating. Whittington stayed by her. "When the others came over, he had to join them," she whispered. "I would have gone too. For all my loves here, if I could have flown with him I would have."

Bernie put water and a handful of the special grain close to her nest. Al brought out half of his breakfast doughnut and crumbled it for her. She closed her eyes. She wouldn't talk. For two days she didn't move except to attend to her necessaries. She ate nothing, drank nothing, said nothing. Even Havey's nosings and lickings got no response.

Whittington started telling stories about her as if she weren't there—how she'd helped him when he'd lost his home. Soon the others joined in. Abby said they were doing the Lady's obituary.

"What's an obituary?" Ben wanted to know.

"What they write about you after you're dead," Abby said.

The Lady opened her eyes.

Ben told about her encouraging his reading. "She taught me about taking charge of myself," he said. The Lady stirred a little at that. The Old One told the story of the truce with the rats.

Abby made them all laugh about the night with the owls. They told one another about her speech the afternoon of the hawk's attack.

"Who will lead in her place?" Wilhelmina asked. "She had standards, she was like a good Dutch aunt. She taught us to keep clean and tidy."

The Lady struggled up. "I am *not* dead," she declared with a tremendous flap. She looked at the sky and flapped again. "Flying isn't everything. There's something to staying put where you're needed."

The animals cheered, even the Old One, who yelled, "Hear! Hear!"

The Lady looked at Wilhelmina.

"I'm Muscovy, I am *not* Dutch!"

# 45

# The Last Warm Afternoon of Autumn

THAT FALL WHITTINGTON and the Lady trained his children. His son was named Fitzwarren; he'd named his daughter Mary Green.

"Before the big snow comes I'm going to take a trip," Whittington announced. "I have to see my boy again, the boy in my home before. The one they sent away. I'm going to take Mary Green to him." Mary Green nodded, as if she'd known all along.

The last warm afternoon of autumn Ben, Abby, the Lady, and Whittington sat out in front of the barn together. Ben knew how to stroke the cat's back to make him stretch and purr with pleasure. His purr was louder now but it was still ragged. Brahms sang to them.

When Ben started talking about the reading lessons, Coraggio, Theo, Wilhelmina, and the horses moseyed over. "It was like coming in out of the dark," he said. "When I started, it was dark, there were shapes and things but nothing was clear. Then it was clear and I could see. It was like being born."

As the sun set, a chill wind came up. They went into the barn to see if his first word was still on the stanchion. It was.

# Endnote

THE RICHARD WHITTINGTON of history was born in Gloucestershire in the west of England in the late 1350s. He was a younger son of a nobleman. It was the custom of the time that the family's wealth went to the firstborn male, so Dick was not rich as a young man. He did have the advantages of name and connections.

He became the richest merchant of his day as a London mercer supplying the gentry with velvets, damasks, and silks. There is a record of his supplying King Henry IV with cloth of gold for his daughter's wedding. He loaned substantial sums to the kings of his time and was three times elected lord mayor of London.

After his wife and daughter died, he decided to devote a large part of his fortune to public charities. The size of his bequests and the fact that most were devoted to aiding the poor led to his becoming a folk hero after his death. Money from his estate founded a college and an almshouse and contributed substantially to repairing St. Bartholomew's Hospital and building a new library at Greyfriars. Other sums went to the rebuilding of Newgate prison because it was "feble, over litel and so contagious of the Eyre, yat hit caused the deth of many men" and to tapping a spring in the bank of the city ditch to make it easy for people to get clean water at that place.

He died in London in 1423.

In the early seventeenth century, Whittington's name, still famous because of his generosities, got attached to a thirteenth-century Persian folktale about an orphan who gained a fortune through his remarkable cat.

A similar legend about a remarkable mouser is attached to the life of a fourteenth-century Italian merchant named Francesco di Marco Datini. See Iris Origo, *The Merchant of Prato* (London: Jonathan Cape, 1957), pages 3–4.

Dick Whittington and his cat first appeared together in a play, now lost, that was licensed in 1605. That same year, "The History of Richard Whittington, of his lowe byrth, his great fortune, as yt was plaied by the pruynces servants" and "The virtuous Lyfe and memorable Death of Sir Richard Whittington, mercer, some-tyme Lord Maiour" were published. Those too have been lost.

The earliest surviving reference to his legend is found in Thomas Heywood's "If you know not me, you know nobody," published in 1606.

The earliest form of the story in the British

Museum Collection is a black-letter ballad of 1641, "London's glory and Whittington's renoun; or a looking glass for the citizens of London; being a remarkable story how Sir Richard Whittington . . . came to be three times Lord Mayor of London, and how his rise was by a cat."

Present-day versions appear in Andrew Lang, ed., *The Blue Fairy Book* (Philadelphia: Macrae Smith Company, 1926); Walter de la Mare, *Animal Stories,* "Whittington and His Cat" (London: Faber and Faber, 1939); and Ronne P. Randall, *Dick Whittington* (London: Penguin, 1993).

Entries for Richard Whittington appear in the *Dictionary of National Biography,* 1900, and *Encyclopedia Britannica,* 11th ed. His era is described in Barbara W. Tuchman, *A Distant Mirror: The Calamitous 14th Century* (New York: Knopf, 1978).

For information about rats, I relied on Martin Hart, *Rats* (London: Allison & Busby, 1982). Rats and the plague are described in Hans Zinsser, *Rats, Lice and History* (New York: Blue Ribbon Books, 1935); Philip Ziegler, *The Black Death* (London: Collins, 1969); and Norman Cantor, *In the Wake of the Plague* (New York: Free Press, 2001).

The fable referred to in chapter 13 is "The Lion and the Rat" by Jean de La Fontaine. I used Brian Wildsmith's edition (New York: Oxford University Press, 1963).

Concerning medieval gardens, plants, and medicines, my authorities were Sir Frank Crisp, *Medieval Gardens* (New York: Hacker Art Books, 1979), a reprint of the 1924 edition; John Harvey, *Early Nurserymen* (London: Phillimore, 1975); and L. H. Bailey, *The Standard Cyclopedia of Horticulture,* 3 vols., 2nd ed. (New York: Macmillan Publishers Limited, 1942).

The *Amapacherie* mentioned in chapter 18 is possibly a euphorbia. The English mercer Peter Collinson described it in a letter to John Ellis, November 24, 1757, as "a wonderfull E. India plant. . . . For a small pebble being wrap'd in its Leaves & held in the mouth for a Small Time it brake into Sand," as quoted in Alan W. Armstrong, ed., *"Forget Not Mee & My Garden . . .": Selected Letters, 1725–1768, of Peter Collinson, F.R.S.* (Philadelphia: American Philosophical Society, 2002).

I studied ducks, chickens, cats, and dogs firsthand. I studied goats firsthand too, and read Daniel Defoe, *Robinson Crusoe;* Jim Corbett, *Goatwalking* (New York: Viking, 1991); and *Encyclopedia Britannica,* 11th edition, "Goats." For more on cats, see Herodotus, *The Persian Wars,* translated by George Rawlinson (New York: Modern Library, 1942).

For information about childhood in medieval England, I relied on Nicholas Orme, *Medieval Children* (New Haven: Yale University Press, 2001), and Barbara

Special thanks to copy editors Artie Bennett, Jenny Golub, Godwin Chu, Alison Kolani, and Susan Goldfarb. The cat came to you in a barnyard way; he is now fit company.

This book owes its life to Martha Armstrong, Alfred Hart, Mary Hill, and Kate Klimo.

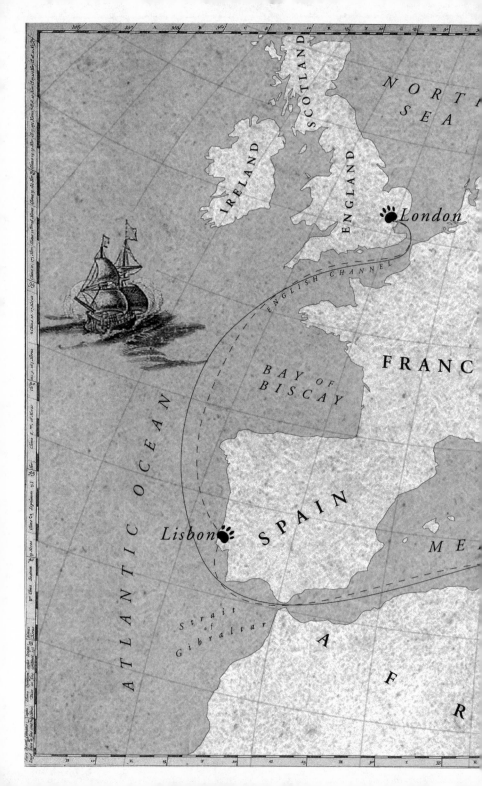

THE HOLY
ROMAN EMPIRE

BYZANTINE
EMPIRE

*ITALY*

BLACK
SEA

*Constantinople*

*Palermo*

*ERRANEAN SEA*

*Tripoli*

C A

KEY

*Dick Whittington's*
*First Voyage*     – – – – –

*Dick Whittington's*
*Second Voyage*     ————